Realized your fantasies

Are dressed up in travesties

Enjoy yourself with no regrets

Supernatural Superserious

R.E.M.

ACKNOWLEDGMENTS

To the early readers who inspired me to release this to the world,
I thank you.

For my talented sister, Stacie Cary, who designed the cover and
graphics.

To the members of R.E.M., your music provided the soundtrack
for my life.

For any man who grapples with love, abandonment, adoration,
regret, disappointment, appreciation, or gratitude from their
father or son, this one goes out to you.

BEGIN THE END
2000 One

Emerging through the Shatzell Avenue door, Drew's middle pudged and his forehead deepened more since they last rendezvoused. He set his bulbous Nokia 3210 on the counter, and ordered a beer. "What a loss for you, my friend; and for this area. Just last winter the Poughkeepsie Journal ran a story about this hotel and quoted him. So sorry."

"Thanks, Drew." That awkward silence crept in, neither knowing where to take the conversation. R.E.M.'s *Fall on Me* crackled through the bar's aging speakers with Michael Stipe's consistent tremble lingering just long enough to trigger a memory, sounding much like the original album Steele wore out on his record player, one of the last vinyl albums he owned before cassettes flooded the stores.

"Drew, *That Night*," gaps in Drew's narrative left Steele quizzing Drew's version of events, "what happened to you?" As a trained historian Steele couldn't assemble the jagged shreds Drew dropped occasionally. "I'm buying tonight," Steele offered and signaled to the bartender another round. Steele figured this moment of reflection on Papa's loss might be the best opportunity to probe Drew for the full version.

1

Drew hesitated. *Fall on Me's* backing vocals instructed him to finally share the totality.

"I'm not much of a storyteller, you know that, but okay." Drew waved his hand to flick a fly off the scruffy bar. "Though I'm much better with stories now than my run-on-sentence high school self." The bartender dropped the frothing glasses in front of them, a pair of drained mugs clinking as she swept them away single-handedly.

"After that fight with Chris I was pissed off. At him—and you." He dug in. "I didn't know what to do after leaving you guys. I wasn't ready to go home, and figured since my parents thought I was away for the night I'd find somewhere to go. I wandered the woods for a while, following the ridge west towards Milan, since you two were heading south. By mid-afternoon all my food was gone, and I didn't have a clue how to find food out there." He sipped the beer, a bland domestic ale with little flavor.

"I decided being out in the woods alone wasn't the best idea. Looking back now I was more scared than I would've admitted then. I was near the golf club, so I headed towards Oriole Mills Road hoping I could hitch a ride with someone passing by. And mosquitos were a bitch." They both forced slight grins, locking eyes for a millisecond.

"Before I reached the road I walked through the burnt cabin. You remember. Half a charred wall; old pull tab cans; some odd pieces of metal, like a frame to those old beach chairs with that sticky plastic tubing we used to fold into triangles and use as forts; a toppled over stove. And..." Drew stopped for a long pull from his glass, staring at his mug to find the next words. Steele wondered if Drew was perhaps reading into the carbonation's pattern for assistance. "And two things that I took. Later I stuck them in my drawer at home, and kept them all these years." From his baggy jeans he pulled a rusted pocket knife and a key. "I think you'd want them."

Nothing struck Steele about either item, the knife something likely to be at a garage sale for a dollar, probably some cheap souvenir. He held the knife up to catch the strongest light in the room, emanating from the yellowed hanging beer sign above the pool table. Gritty to open, just a single two and a half inch locking skinner blade, the handle crafted from cow horn covering only one side. "Why would I want them?"

"Look here," Drew pointed to the bolster at the blade's base.

Lady Liberty stared at Steele from the blade. "Beautiful," Steele admitted. He began to question the authenticity and possible story behind the knife. The bolster read Shrade, USA.

"Check the other side, too."

The bartender noticed Steele squinting hard, coming over with a lighter. "Thanks—and another round please." She nodded, her tight black ponytail swaying as she moved down the counter to pour. Flicking the lighter and holding it near the knife two etched letters emerged. JS.

Drew swilled the last of his warm beer, pushed the glass forward and pulled the next one close. "I also saw letters carved on the remnants of the wall. Not full words, some moss had grown over parts." With a pen from his pocket and a Rollicking Ale coaster he sketched:

JA TEE

"I'm guessing it's your Jacob's knife. That's his initials on the knife, and his name carved in the wall. Look." He filled in the missing letters.

JA cob s TEE le

Steele doubted Drew's claim. Why would he live in a cabin, so close to the house? When was he there? Steele speculated, "those letters can be many other names. Jack, James, Jared, Jason...Teemer, Teeps, Steem." Without more evidence Steele dismissed Drew's suggestion. "Let me see the key." Turning it over Steele dismissed that too. Not much to it although an irregular oblong shape, ridged along the middle, a tad rusted. "Ever try it in anything?"

Drew shifted his glance between his beer mug, the clock, and the slender bartender. "Kind of an odd shaped, isn't it?" Drew poked the key in Steele's hand, hastily stood up and started towards the men's room. Natalie Merchant reminded the friends over the ailing speakers that the night is theirs together, covering the Springsteen/Smith classic *Because the Night* in an acoustic version, as Drew headed towards the dingiest part of the downtrodden inn. Steele reflected on beer as he inspected the key waiting for Drew. Such an intricate process to brew, ferment, filter, bottle, ship, store, and sell: all to be expelled down a crusty urinal in this dismal bar.

"Of course, what happened at crazy Betty's house you won't believe," Drew dropped, then gulped half the remaining beer, still standing. "That's another part of the story you've never heard. But tonight's not the time to tell it." Drew massaged Steele's shoulders with one firm pulse. "See you at the service tomorrow."

"Drew, man, thanks for coming. Don't forget those things," he scooped up the knife and key.

"No, they're yours. I've had'm too long."

***

Earlier that day Steele searched old magazines stacked like Dutch pillars in Papa's house. *LIFE* from the 1950's, *National Geographic* issues spanning decades, shockingly even some early issues of *Playboy*. He thought he knew all Papa's quirks and subtleties, but these bare-all rags predated Steele's appearance in the world. Papa never alluded to anything sexual in all their shared years.

In one earmarked, ragged issue of *LIFE* Steele scanned an ad for a "Man-Sized Pen, specifically made for the hand of a man." He envisioned that pen in Papa's hand, the hand that both disciplined and fed him, the hand now gone.

Rummaging random boxes in the attic, Steele rescued a wax-sealed envelope from among an abandoned stash of hippie skirts, his formal names neatly printed in unfamiliar yet vaguely intimate handwriting, **Thurgood Levi Steele.** Who wrote this, and why had it remained tucked away in musty women's clothes? The pulse of masculine energy sizzled in the Steele household, no woman ever sharing space under their roof in his lifetime.

He uncovered dozens of pictures of a carnival, a mid-century county fair, images with dull hues by standards of the year 2000, yet the yellow/green contrasts differentiated foliage more so than the sharper, clearer pictures of modern magazines with their advanced inks and superior paper composition. Those were simpler times to live in, Papa repeated, with simpler rules to build relationships. Papa's passion for the past intensified with each extinguished decade; he often spoke of a time machine to transport him to the days of Dutch settlement in the region, where he would build a homestead with his hands and heart.

Steele's research on whether territorial claims of the late 1600s Hudson Valley may have reflected familial lands division patterns of contemporaneous Friesland remained incomplete due to a dearth of credible sources—and Steele found several promising volumes among Papa's library. With near reverence for the rarity of the volumes Steele handled the books with gloved hands, gently placing them in a box for his inspection at the university. Other classifications emerged as he filtered the treasures—for the Rhinebeck Public Library, the Red Hook Public Library, and the Hudson Valley Historical Society. Normally he'd be ecstatic at the glimpse of history in these volumes; but Steele's world had been flattened, the thrills of learning and the slow mound-building process of knowledge creation bulldozed by Papa's death.

MEMORIAL MESS
2000 Two

Darryl, sporting a blue blazer two sizes small and three days of gray stubble ringing his face, plopped his bulk beside Steele. "Well ain't that just the shit. Old man's done gone and died. Sorry, pal."

"Mind speaking a little quieter, Mr. Cooper? We're not in the woods. How's Alice?"

"Alive. Takin' care of the grandkids now, and a couple neighbor kids too." Steele feared Darryl's voice carried to the back of the chapel, disturbing mourners.

Steele received other acquaintances. Despite Papa's diminishing attendance at community events in recent years, town commissioners, historical society members, orchard owners, festival judges, and even The Observer's reporter appeared for the memorial service.

The previous mayor—twice removed—reminisced with Steel how Papa quickly embarked on soliloquies to anyone unfortunate to ask him about the town's history. Lining the eastern edge of the expansive Hudson River for several miles, he would list off the tracts once owned by the families of Schuyler, Beekman, Livingston, and their contemporaries' massive homes with breathtaking river views. From Tivoli's early ice harvesting and wool production industries to its current artists' enclave Papa could, and would for the poor souls that dared open the topic with him, spin tales beginning with Dutch settlers to the bastardization of his town as a bedroom community for IBMers circling to Kingston daily like homing pigeons. Papa's listeners, if they could pay attention long enough, would hear that the town's most significant historical claim may or may not have occurred there, the rumored 1804 arrest of Vice President Aaron Burr after fatally wounding Alexander Hamilton in their duel. For generations locals speculated the imprecise location as the grounds between the middle school and high school—land once owned by Papa and his ancestors.

Drew settled beside Steele, the familiarity of long-standing friendship a comfort to Steele. Papa opted for cremation, with burial beneath an apple tree—a Belle de Boskoop tree, a large Dutch early harvest cultivar with unpredictably yellow, green, or red fruit.

Steele welcomed the attendees from the rostrum, and drew papers from inside his jacket. Murmurs subsided as he began. The crowd's size comforted Steele, who dreaded an empty hall. "As we gather here, Papa surely would appreciate the show of support. I hope we reflect on his life, his passions, and celebrate the eclectic man we each knew in some unique manner." He scanned the room, relaxed his shoulders as he would when beginning a lecture to students, and launched into the service.

"Those who knew Papa would testify to his need for control. Rather than leave to chance the comments made at his memorial he wrote his own eulogy." Muffled laughs rippled softly through the room, heads nodding in agreement.

"Stand up!" Puzzled faces stared at Steele, he motioned for them to rise and returned to the prepared ceremony. Reading verbatim Steele forged ahead.

"As you rise, you join with the saints who stand around the throne of God. We offer a prayer to St. Charles Borromeo, Patron Saint of both Apple Orchards and Against Ulcers. Oh, St. Charles Borromeo; the irony of your dedications. Bless the sweet nectar of apples, crisp and nutritious, aiding our health and well-being, warding off evil demons of overactive stomach acid. We stand in the tradition of ages, to respect your elevation over the dastardly apple that tempted Eve (though scholars admit the pomegranate likely seduced the seducer)." Steele glared out at the mourners, drew a breath and mustered resolve to go on. "The Church's blatant hypocrisy to nurture the seed of its evil casts shadows on all the Church's teachings. St. Charles Borromeo, bless this town's wealth and sooth its people's digestive woes." Steele scanned the room, noting reddening faces of the pious, amused smirks sprinkled around the room, and apologetically furrowed his forehead.

"Sit down!" Steele boomed.

The mourners obeyed.

"In your more receptive posture you listen more attentively, more passively, to the man in front of you. No women, of course, not for the Catholics. Rather than a scripture reading for you today, listen to the rhyme from the book of Levi:

> Entered this world to a fam'ly of farm,
> And leave my lot, do I, among my kin,
> Descendants dual strong of mind, strong of arm,
> Daring to merge, announcement forthcomin'.
> Learned of gods, prayer in action, reconcile,
> Truant one gifted me blessing in flesh,
> Lesson born of secret, self witness trial,
> Inward forgiveness, outwardly refresh.
> Solo journey, bolster, elevate all,
> Heart envelops hope, hope envelops heart,
> Return to land, apples to eat, nightfall,
> Daybreak optimism: spirited art.
> Give up, stay down, battle lost, gone goodbye,
> Drop low, descend, required to soar high."

Steele paused, Papa's autobiographical sonnet offering a final insight, adding to the legions of life lessons he sprinkled over the decades. He scanned the room again, noting for the first time his old teacher Betty among the crowd; her creased and craggy face now tattooed a vivid green zebra pattern. Steele finished Papa's message, "If anyone would like to speak, please come forward."

Darryl rose, huffed up the three gentle steps to the platform, released a sigh of exertion, and began. "Well, ain't this just the shit. Ol' Levi done some good in this world, left us the festival, land for the high school, done raised this boy right," pointing at Steele with his sausage-sized thumb, "not that other one, wherever he gone to. We sure is glad we had Levi in our lil' place we call home. That's all I got to—."

"THE TIGRESS SPEAKS" Betty roared, crouched on all fours at the rear of the small chapel's aisle, her emerald eyes glowing; thinning, dyed jet-black hair wildly flailing.

Drew bristled beside Steele. Steele's shoulders tensed, school days' snatches of Tigress conversations flashed back to him.

Betty purred, "In utero Tigress foresaw this boy...now man. Roiling beneath surface, confusion. Sonnet clear...listen dear...holy prayer...broken father...broken son...redemption comes...." Steele and Drew jumped to intervene, to cut off her confused pronouncements, but she reared over them. "ENGAGE with the DIVINE...path emerges to each seeker...pomp and tradition waylay the masses...inner peace a solitary experience."

"Ain't this just the shit. Who let the ol' batty hag in?" Darryl's voice trumped hers, "I'll git her outta here." His hunting instinct carelessly throttled him forward, oblivious to the steps, timbering his trunk and snapping the wooden floorboards when he crashed. He grabbed for his leg screaming "MY GODDAMNED ANKLE! AIN'T THAT JUST THE SHIT!"

Betty/Tigress sprang five yards in one leap, nestled atop the tumbled giant, purred and licked his eyes. "In pain...find comfort." She collapsed atop him.

Town commissioners fled through the back door, the mayor called 9-1-1 from his Nokia Communicator, women shrieked a whirlwind of panic. Steele separated Betty from Darryl, attempting futilely to revive her.

Reading the article the next day, Steele suspected Papa grinned with satisfaction at the memorial's milieu. The beat reporter snapped photos, published as a front-page fiasco headlined *Staid Memorial Erupts Into Chaotic Carnival.*

FIDLER'S BRIDGE
1982

"Eat your spinach, it'll put hair on your chest," Papa instructed Steele.

"But Papa, I don't want hair on my chest," he protested. Papa forced Steele to sit and stare at the slimy green vegetables that were 'good for you'. Hours passed while Steele refused the food, a battle of wills raging silently. Papa cleaned up the pots and pans, read the results of the local high school sports, then listened to a Yankees' game crackle from the AM sports radio station as Steele stubbornly refused the green goop. Some nights Papa listened to a game on that old radio even if the game were being broadcast on TV, never taking Steele's advice to watch the TV instead. Images strengthen the mind, Papa declared.

What Papa didn't see in the battle between boy and vegetable, while quite revoltingly obvious to Steele, was how the overcooked greens slid down his throat, the imagined pains in his stomach, and the agony of the whole experience. No. That glob would never enter Steele's body, not through his free will.

As the seventh inning approached in the Bronx, Papa began to glare Steele's direction with the disapproving look mastered by raising another boy almost twenty years earlier.

Steele sensed the intensity of Papa's burning eyes ignite with the seventh inning stretch. Steele knew too well that if the spinach did not disappear by the ninth inning he would struggle to sit on the school bus in the morning. He gave in, thought of peanuts and Cracker Jacks, forced the spinach down and chased it with warm milk. Better spinach than the belt. But not by much.

Regardless of his performance at the dinner table, Papa shared a story every night. One of Steele's favorites involved an old fisherman catching a huge fish—and before the proud man reached the shore sharks devoured the trophy. It was an easy story to fall asleep to.

Around his ninth birthday Papa first narrated Steele a centuries-old tale that imprinted Steele like a brand. An event turned story, story morphed to tale, and tale cemented to local lore. The kind of story tattooed over an entire community. Of a tragic event long, long ago; a haunting story repeated around bonfires and backyards, breakfasts and bedtimes. Newcomers became ensorcelled by the myth's retelling in its infinite variations, baptism to the town.

Papa began, "Even in those days the city's growing reputation extended well beyond its official limits. Traders from England and Holland met French and Indians. Rutted roads connected us to Boston and Philadelphia, and rough trails tangled up the Hudson to the network of trading outposts at Albany and beyond.

"Midway between New Amsterdam and Albany settlers conquered the hills and valleys, growing food and hunting game; honoring the traditions of the lands they left.

"Parents arranged marriages for their children, often matching a child your age, or younger, to their future wife or husband. Children knew whom they would marry, and on occasions such as weddings or funerals or harvest celebrations they slyly peeked at their future spouses from safe distances.

"One farmer named Staats promised his daughter to marry the son of a farmer half a day's journey south, to Mr. Van Buren's boy.

"The Van Buren Boy was pleased with the hardworking Staats Girl. Her lovely straw colored hair balanced eyes as blue as the magical river; she embodied the land and water the Boy loved. He was convinced she would produce fine sons for him just as her family's farm produced enough food to share with families that might have gone hungry. Like his.

"Thoughts of marrying the scrawny, dim-witted Van Buren Boy ravaged the Staats Girl for months. Her head churned faster than the twirling devil winds that ruined Van Meer's farm one wild August. How could her parents expect her to marry a person she barely knew, whose family squandered the little money eked off their tiny farm?

"Regardless, the wedding day finally approached. Word of mouth invitations passed to families, friends, and disliked neighbors equally. People from as far away as a day's travel attended.

"Women prepared a feast of mutton and beef. Men brewed the strong spirits reserved for celebrating major life events. Musicians journeyed to entertain with whimsy and songs.

"To the Staats Girl's dread, the day arrived to be wed by the poor, weak Van Buren Boy—the senseless fool with little wealth since his father squandered much in frequent visits down south.

"Joy overwhelmed the Van Buren Boy. The Staats Girl had grown prettier each year. He resolved to rebuild his father's losses and prove his worth to her, in time.

"Dressed in white, she felt black would be more appropriate. Her father led her down the aisle, the Staats Bride at the Van Buren Groom's side, gloom clouding her eyes. She prayed for a miracle to save her from her doomed future, yet she had barely blinked and the ceremony ended.

"Plentiful food, raucous music, tiring dancing, flowing drink filled the hundreds gathered in celebration. The previous year's ideal growing season blessed the celebration with exceptional wine. Old men could not remember any better in their time in the New World. The Minister swore it surpassed the water-turned-wine of Jesus's making, some of the best God ever shared with meek humans.

"The Groom took fondly to the sweet wine on his night, more than he ever downed before. He drank until the music stopped and celebrants slept where they dropped.

"The enthusiastic fiddle player, a simple man in his late twenties with a bushy red beard and bulging, honest eyes, packed his instrument to start his journey home in the light of the newly waning moon. He also had indulged in many cups of sweet wine, causing him to take short breaks along his trek.

"The Van Buren Groom, noticing the fiddler's departure, followed to thank him one last time. With the unfamiliar shadows of night and a dizzy head, the Groom's foot wedged under a root. Gray veins of maple bark rushed forward.

"The Staats Bride hid most of the evening, appearing just enough so as not to trigger curiosity. She despondently watched her thin Groom's joyous drinking and dancing, sinking deeper into depression. As her new spouse chased the fiddler she crept a short distance behind them, unnoticed.

"Seeing her scraggy Groom fallen and unmoving, with the fiddler not far ahead, the answer to her prayer seemed obvious.

"She found an iron bar, silently chased the fiddler and collided the rod with his skull as he paused to pee. His legs crumbled, crashing his head on a jutting rock above a slight ravine. She kicked his body, now smiling as it tumbled to the bottom, stopping with his face submerged in the creek beneath the small footbridge that led towards his home.

"She quickly turned back to her snoring Groom and placed the bloodied bar near his left hand.

"That night, and the rest of her life, the Staats Girl slept deeper than the fiddler she murdered, at peace, never to become the Van Buren Wife."

Steele wondered, "Is that the end?"

Papa shook his head and continued. "Shouts of angry men shocked the Van Buren Groom from his rough sleep, quickly approaching him with shovels, hoes, sticks, and rocks. His head pounded, his stomach roiled, his clothes felt gummy from vomit. A sticky paste of mud and blood matted his hair. He scrambled to stand, but stumbled again on the gnarled roots.

"The crowd tied a rope to a branch of the tree above him. Rallied by the Minister the posse shouted KILL THE KILLER and GOD FORGIVE HIM and LET HIM SUFFER FOR HIS

SIN and AN EYE FOR AN EYE.

"Seconds later the Van Buren Groom took his last breath, never to be a Husband."

Young Steele pictured the bloody scene, an innocent man dangling lifeless surrounded by a shouting crowd with another man drowned in a creek. And somewhere nearby the girl peacefully resting.

Papa continued, "To this day, Thurgood, the Fiddler's spirit dwells near that bridge, playing during the waning moon for those whose ears might be open. He plays for the soul of the wrongly killed Groom, he plays for his own family, and he plays because music brought him the greatest joy of his short life. And, some say, he plays to heal and forgive."

"Is it true, Papa? Does he really exist? Can you really hear his music?" the boy asked earnestly.

"Faith has no limits, my boy."

STAY, UP
1987, June

To fight boredom Steele ventured in the woods alone, stopping in a spot he, Chris, and Drew usually leapt over on the way to the charred cabin a couple miles into the woods. The trickling water of the creek beside him normally dried by the end of May, but heavy winter snows and a late thaw pushed the water forward to June. Oblivious to the stream's soothing incantations, R.E.M.'s pounding *I Believe* drilled his eardrums from the Walkman while the rainbows of greens and browns surrounding him clashed in harmony.

He picked his way out of that speckle on the planet, passing skunk cabbage at the swamp's edge and crushing seedlings underfoot that sprang up on the trails Papa voluntarily maintained with others from the neighborhood. Land ownership, Papa constantly repeated, created oppression and disparity among groups of people; a tool of the elite to control the masses. Just like organized religion, he would add.

On his return Steele passed by the deli for an Italian ice and cola, soaking the top of the frozen treat with the soda until it became slushy, scraping off a layer using the supplied wooden spoon and hoping not to get a splinter in his tongue. As he savored the fizz and froth, he thought of a backwoods guy from his carpentry class who invited him to a Youth of Catholicism club. The group retreated to a majestic monastery on the west side of the Hudson River, with unending views of undulating hills boasting pale greens of adolescent leaves which Steele inhaled during the prescribed silence, covertly listening to R.E.M.'s *Dead Letter Office*. The eclectic compilation of oddities, unreleased album offcuts, and song fragments teased Steele with hopes of another, more uniform sounding album soon. He studied the tape's liner notes for insights to spiritual guidance, rather than the Bible verses suggested by the priest.

Drew's father drove by after a workday with the cable company, dropping Drew off. None of Steele's friends could tell him what their fathers did for their jobs; they just knew what type of company they worked in. More than Steele knew of Jacob.

"How was practice?" Steele asked Drew rotely.

"Y'know." Drew smirked ambivalently. Steele never believed Drew liked running, he never placed above fifth in any competition. Steele despised running, and most forms of physical competition defeated him, despite lanky limbs and physical agility. "There's a party at the DeTrombos tomorrow night their parents went to the city Chris told me about it are you going?"

"I have to ask Papa first." Chris and his brother enjoyed a curfew of two, and Drew had no curfew. Papa forced Steele home early, by ten, much before any party really started booming, "to protect the family's reputation," as Papa justified the rule. What reputation, Steele wondered, but the belt loomed in the closet and Steele complied.

Papa balanced his book on a precarious stack beside him and peered over the top of his wire-rimmed glasses, emphasizing his resemblance to Ronald Reagan ringed with tufts of blondish graying curls. "Now, why would you want to do that? Ten is plenty late for a fellow your age."

"Drew doesn't have to go home, his parents let him stay out as late as he wants." Steele repeated the reason like a bird's futile efforts pecking at its reflection in a mirror.

"As I've told you before, once school is over you can stay longer." He reached for his book, *Saints: Deities or Demigods.*

"But I don't finish dishwashing until almost ten, that's no time to get to their house." Steele faded, knowing that school ended next week and the curfew extension awaited. And whining irked Papa, which always backfired. "Is the curfew going to be eleven?"

"There will be no curfew," he stated nonchalantly without removing his eyes from the page. "You're old enough now to govern yourself."

A fever of disbelief crossed Steele's forehead. His ears rang with exhilaration, and he grew an inch in that moment.

Papa leaned forward and peered towards him, almost through him; Steele felt like Papa wasn't even looking at him any longer, like Papa gazed at a memory—reliving a dreaded flash in time. Snapping back he spoke again. "Telling this to Jacob was the closest I've come to regretting anything, Thurgood. He abused the freedom I granted him, and never learned how to control his actions. It saddens me deeply that you could not grow under his guidance; I believe he could have matured to raise you." He stopped, lingering in a lost moment. "I'm eternally grateful that we remain together, Thurgood."

Damn, Papa could cut down a high! Why bring up Jacob, again? He dumped Steele like a t-shirt that became too small. He's gone and forgotten. Steele wished Papa would never mention that name again.

***

Gleaming in the morning sun on top of the gymnasium roof at school the next day sat the temporary gargoyle, the peak of senior pranks, with Class of '87 hastily spray-painted along the side of the VW Beetle. Steele marveled at how the anonymous bandits heaved the powder blue body thirty-five feet up, undetected. This freakish feat one-upped the sparkly painted kegs dangling like monstrous, drunken Christmas ornaments inside the gym the year before.

Rather than dismantle the body piecemeal, the entire janitorial staff shoved it over the edge; Steele admired the rotation like an oversized football as it plummeted. Rumors buzzed all day about who possessed the savvy talent and access to tools. With their party later that night, and a dozen years of proven mischief, the DeTrombo twins topped the list.

Gossip over the prank, and speculation about whether there would be more, continued at the Youth of Catholicism meeting the following week. Papa insisted on attending church and sending Steele to Sunday school while he grew. The rote recitation of prayers; kneeling and standing and sitting in unchanging order mystified Steele. The actions threaded Steele to traditions older and deeper and larger than himself, Father Seamus explained, rituals rooted hundreds or thousands of years distant that held symbolic significance. But that meant as much to Steele as ice tea to a polar bear.

FAIR WORK, CHANCE CRASH
1987, August

Red Hook, New York schooled Steele; Rhinebeck raised him. Rednecks and conservative mentality steeped Red Hook. Rhinebeck featured artists and Manhattan's refugees. Rhinebeck's art house—a single screen, sixty-year-old theatre— contrasted Red Hook's six picture multiplex. Red Hook's pay-by-the-week motel paled beside Rhinebeck's oldest continuously run inn in America, rumored to once shelter George Washington. Rhinebeck hosted the second largest fair in the state; Red Hook offered a weekly hardscrabble flea market. Red Hook's trailer parks barked at Rhinebeck's subdued artists' colonies. The Old Rhinebeck Aerodrome, known regionally for its vivid, antique bi-plane and triplane shows, covertly hid behind Red Hook's boundary—but wouldn't admit it.

Rhinebeckers envied Red Hook's Devout Bovine Ice Cream. The owner coached the high school girls' volleyball team to multiple state championships over most of the late 1980s and early 1990s; its lush and smooth and bold ice cream made on premises, with prices locked at 1979 levels. Families of four enjoyed lavish sundaes or gigantic milkshakes, and drove home with change from a ten-dollar bill.

Like a desert flower the Dutchess County Fairgrounds lay dormant in Rhinebeck most of the year. The fair exploded its glorious gaudiness for six days each August, dwarfed only by the New York State Fair in Syracuse. Rhinebeckers split on whether the fair sparkled as the premier prize of the town, or erupted as the herpes of the village's crotch. Red Hook offered nothing remotely comparable, to the relief of every resident.

Rhinebeck attracted Steele like a magnet attracting its opposite.

***

With the sweet taste of cream and sugar in his mouth for the first time that summer, summer of *That Night*, Steele jumped on his bike to pedal the back roads towards Rhinebeck to meet Drew and search for odd jobs with vendors at the upcoming county fair. Papa cautioned him against it, especially warning about the carnies, but Steele insisted on earning some money at the fair. Steele nagged for weeks until Papa relented and lifted his punishment.

Burly men unfurled masses of machinery from precisely packed trailers, turning mundane metal cubes into thrilling curves. Food vendors connected water and waste pipes, filled Frialators and soda fountains to prepare for the hordes while Drew hunted for a weeklong job. The boys peddled vendor to vendor begging for tasks like hauling, lifting, stacking—anything. Ultimately they returned home with empty stomachs and empty pockets. All the workers told Drew that at thirteen he was too young to work.

Mrs. Lasby, the secretary from the principal's office, had offered Steele a job at the apple fritter booth a few weeks before school ended. Her lion's mane, dyed scarlet, piled high and wide cemented with a quarter can of hairspray juxtaposed her aging face, seeding endless jokes among his classmates; but Steele regarded her as kind and undeserving of such abuses. She told him that his reputation as a hard working, quiet boy with strong grades and deep local family history prompted her to offer him the fritter booth job. Whatever, Steele thought; it'll be great money!

Late the second morning of the fair, as families started to trickle in, Mrs. Lasby directed Steele, "Thurgood, please go to the van for more trays. Take the dolly with you. Thanks, Sweetie." She always called everyone Sweetie, or Dumplin', or some other saccharin name that Steele dismissed.

Tromping through the fairgrounds back to the fritter booth with the burdened cart overwhelmed Steele's senses. The muses of county fair fare distracted him: fat-laden air of fried corn dogs and fried dough; the lights shouting their rainbow cacophony of messages; the game masters luring young and old to try their luck on the dime throws or tossing a ping pong ball to win a goldfish; the mechanical clunking and subsequent shrills on the rides. Looking over the rides, he plotted out which ones would tempt his fate during breaks.

The metal dolly stopped abruptly, spilling boxes. Tall and lanky, tanned brown, in a red t-shirt and overalls, a man cursed more over thirty seconds than Steele heard in a typical day of school. His voice sounded young, like everything about him changed in puberty but the hormones skipped his vocal chords. "What the fuck you doin' kid? Watch where the fuck you goin'. You damn near broke my shin. You blind, boy?" His green eyes peered from under a cap, wild hair flipping out from beneath the edges.

"No, I'm not blind. I, I...," Steele stuttered, "I'm sorry. I was looking at the rides and..." he shook with fear under the towering man, an urge to flee gripping him.

"You better not go knockin' into none of them other guys," he wagged a greasy finger in the direction of the roller coaster, "They'll knock you upside the head with that cart a'yours. Then you'll know what hit you. Get the fuck out of here, greenie," he squeaked.

Late that night Papa picked Steele up cruising the back, unpaved road. Steele told him of the incident, of the cursing man with a high-pitched voice, which Steele replayed in his mind while peeling apples and dunking batter-dipped slices in boiling oil for ten hours that August day.

Papa asked a dozen questions about the guy, none that Steele could answer. What was so interesting about this guy, Steele wondered, but exhaustion blocked his desire to speak. Steele imagined the clogged two-lane road connecting Red Hook and Rhinebeck, relieved that Papa knew this rat route home.

Steele considered himself fortunate to work the fair that summer. Lucky to be allowed outside at all. After *That Night*, just two months earlier, Papa cut him off from leaving the house. He banned Drew from visiting. No phone calls. And Chris, of course—should he somehow reappear—could never approach Steele again.

FECKLESS VARIATIONS
1987, June

Steel and Drew armed themselves for the annual Water War through Red Hook's streets and alleys on the last day of school.

Most boys armed themselves with the latest aquatic weaponry, as well as ubiquitous water balloons. The weapon of desire was the Super Drencher XT-6000, the most powerful water cannon outside of the garden hose. Commercials boasted a range of fifty feet and it held one full gallon. The vengeful jocks, who Steele generally avoided, colored their water with permanent dye; a couple blonde boys entered high school that fall still bearing trace remnants of the Water War in their hair.

Drew struggled to describe his acquisition to Steele, "the XT, can, like y'know, hit a tree fifty feet away with the wind blowing in all directions while the user is blindfolded riding in the bed of a pickup with two flat tires and a dog driving after a cat in a dense forest at night." Steele couldn't understand how Drew passed English class.

The standard translucent yellow water pistol bought at Minter's Pharmacy for 89¢ served Steele adequately. Enough to signal he would play while in truth his enthusiasm for the Water War ticked in just one notch above his yearning for boiled spinach. The pistol squirted for an hour until it developed a leak, then he tossed on the side of the road like an apple core.

Drew and Steele dodged balloons, waylaid people from behind then sprinted from sight, and became the targets of several ambushes in retaliation. Waterlogged and hungry, they eventually turned up at Chris's porch. Chris avoided the Water War to laze instead.

Chris lay stretched on his deck beside his circular above ground swimming pool. He soaked in the warm sun of the early summer afternoon drinking cold cherry cola and eating soft chocolate chip cookies. A large, half eaten bag of Cheezey Oodles lay beside him. His Depeche Mode *Black Celebration* tape seeped from the boom box near the cooler.

"I don't like this synth music," Steele shared while settling into a lounge chair, "I'd rather hear real physical instruments than artificial keyboards."

"Keyboards, synth, and sampling give them more options for interesting sounds," Chris defended his music.

"Give me some Cheezey Oodles," Drew demanded, diverting them from their endless debate over musical styles.

"Get 'em yourself. Anything you want, go ahead," Chris offered, waving his hand dismissively.

The drawn out mechanical musical and moaning vocal style irritated Steele, but he honored their unstated rule that the host chose the music. They avoided Drew's house, his preference for big hair bands ranked below synth pop to Steele.

From music they ventured to the Yankees—a topic they all agreed on—to vacations plans for summer to the new family moving in down the street.

During a pause in chatter, Steele wandered into versions of the fiddler's story. "Drew, your father's family goes back nearly as far as mine. Didn't you say the Groom got jealous and drunk then killed the fiddler for trying to seduce the Bride during the celebration?"

"Yeah, and they both die and the fiddler plays for the girl until she joins him forever," Drew finished.

Chris asked, "Do you think it's true, the fiddler? Why are there so many versions? We didn't have stories like that in Binghamton." Since Steele first told Chris the story, he asked

Steele about it nearly every day.

"Well," Steele mumbled and paused, "Papa usually exaggerates his stories, but he knows about this area. He reads a lot of books, especially local history." Drew and Steele shifted in chairs around a weather-stained table crunching on nacho chips. Chris continued to lounge, feet out, Depeche Mode eerily stretching from the speakers. "Yeah, I suppose there's some truth. Why?"

"We should go check it out. The full moon was last night," Chris teased.

The draw of adventure tugged at Steele.

"But," objected Drew nervously, "there's no way our parents will let us go there, it's twenty miles from here by road, none of us drive, my bike's broken, and I'm supposed to be at another summer camp next week in the Catskills to learn how to appreciate the wondrous beauty of nature or something hokey like that."

"You scared, Thomas? If so, stay home. I've never seen or heard a ghost, I wanna check it out. We don't have much to do this week," Chris challenged him mischievously.

Steele bristled when Chris used Drew's real first name. They called each other by their last names, unless challenging each other or to pick a fight. Drew's real names were Thomas Andrews; Chris's parents named him James Christander at birth. Steele's given name, Thurgood, embarrassed him and he much preferred Steele. Steele sounded so strong and macho, Thurgood too bookish and nerdy.

The challenge hung among them. In the silence a deep voiced shout carried from three houses down, cut short by a thud and sharp scream. "The Buzzwolds at it again," Chris commented, "probably have another kid by the end of winter."

Drew gazed toward the porch's lumber as if they might supply his answer to dissuade Chris. Steele jumped in, "It probably doesn't exist. I've heard so many versions—the wedding version, the version where the fiddler left a baptism; another one when the fiddler was caught with a guy's daughter."

"But they all end the same, right? Fiddler falls, or gets shoved or whatever, and plays his music near the bridge. So, Thomas and Thurgood," Chris prodded the dragon, "do you want to go find Fiddler's Bridge and see if it's true?"

Steele sensed a melodic message, like words mimicked on strings, nothing like he'd ever heard in his world; the meaning came over eras and through ether to whisper *Yes. Yes, come. It's time.* More of a sensation than a sound, a prophetic tingle. Steele dismissed the whatever-it-was. "I'll go, why not? No more curfew!"

Drew simply nodded unconvincingly, throwing his gaze to the two by fours of the pool deck, a look Steele knew to be Drew's submission, a look Steele had seen since the first grade.

SAINTS AND LIES
1987, June

Steele raced home after Chris's house for Papa's for the end-of-school-year meal tradition, which Papa's mother cooked for him on the last day of his school years too: a deep, moist chocolate cake with chocolate frosting and chocolate sprinkles, marinated grilled steak, and baked potatoes, in that order. Nothing green.

After dinner Papa and Steele strolled around the neighborhood, shadows stretching for night's arrival. Along the walk Papa stopped to shake hands with a neighbor walking his dogs. The man briefly gripped Steele's shoulder, then continued on with his Dalmatians.

Papa turned to Steele to say that that man was an untrustworthy fellow.

"How do you know?" Steele asked, wondering how Papa knew so much about people since he spent nearly all his time reading and alone.

"When you offer your hand to a man, a good man with nothing to hide, no secrets hanging about him, that man will put the web of skin between his thumb and forefinger firmly against your web. He will wrap his fingers around the bottom of your hand and shake from the elbow. His wrist will remain stiff, and even if he is not a strong man, his concentration will be in the palm of your hand. You will feel not only his grip, but also a certain warmth exuding from his palm into your own, the connection will be more than physical.

"Thurgood, as your hands meet, your eyes should find his. You'll look into his eyes and see his being, read the true nature of his character. Is he a fool with shallow eyes or a thinker with old, deep eyes? A light-hearted soul with lively, bright eyes or a mysterious person with cloudy eyes? An untrustworthy man with eyes that won't meet yours or a lonely man with brooding eyes? The old adage is true, Thurgood, eyes cannot lie."

Papa and Steele continued in silence, or as silent as a suburban neighborhood can be. A lawnmower purred in the distance, leaves rustled with the moving air, chained dogs barked at the pair passing by. Steele concentrated on the rhythm of their footsteps, three of his for every two of Papa's.

When they returned to their house Steele told Papa that he planned to camp with Drew and Chris. Steele nervously rushed his explanation, "We'll hike through the cornfield past Millerd's Pond into the woods. I'm bringing a tent, sleeping bag, flashlight, and some food. Drew has his sleeping bag and mosquito repellant and food. Chris can borrow a sleeping bag from his sister and bring food, junk food most likely, and a tent. Everyone will bring water." He avoided Papa's hazel green eyes, so similar to his own.

"I don't like the idea of you boys going out alone, but you're old enough to camp one night. You can go, but do me one favor. Take this prayer card with you." He reached into his desk drawer and pulled out what looked like a colorful business card. "This is a card of St. Christopher, the patron saint of travelers. He'll watch over you to be sure you remain safe."

Steele took it out of respect for the old man, and to avoid an argument. Papa's knowledge of the saints, the Catholic pantheon of gods and goddesses as he referred to them, rivaled his encyclopedic familiarity with local history. Whether Papa actually believed in saints, prayed to them, or entertained a fascination with hypocritical Catholic beliefs in one God while also offering prayers to minor deities, Steele never resolved before Papa's passing.

Papa named the saint for everything, whenever he could. Plants, animals, children, procreation, alcohol, communication, throats. There was probably even a patron saint of marshmallows, Steele suspected. Saint Dral of 12th century France, a man that dedicated his life to the undying theory that a squishy, white ball created from sugar, gelatin, and oil would alleviate the burden of hunger for the peasants of his day.

Papa's shelves boasted volumes on the lives of the saints, what they represented to the average layman, where and when they lived, how they distinguished themselves, and which pope canonized them.

Papa never spoke much to Steele of God, Jesus, or the other bigwigs of the Church. He acknowledged their existence by attending mass on major holidays and a few saint feast days—yet another line of proof to him that Catholicism modeled itself on Greek, Roman, and pagan polytheistic traditions. Steele made sense of Papa's beliefs by thinking of Papa's beliefs as a slow simmering soup where water was God, Jesus flavored the broth and saints filled out textures and random bits of goodness in the bottom of the bowl.

***

On the anniversary of Grandma Lilli's death Papa retrieved her rosary beads and hiked into the woods with Steele. Grandma Lilli and Papa prayed the rosary together a few times per week, he once mentioned to Steele. In the many years since her death he only prayed to them during the walking meditation in the woods to be nearer to her.

***

Despite his preference for R.E.M. over religion Steele agreed to go with Papa to church simply to get out of the house the summer of *That Night*.

RELUCTANT RECRUIT
1972, August

"I gonna have me a baby at home, I can't be leavin' it and the mom." Jake rejected Ranger's offer.

"We'll take care a ya. No worries. Give you a place to sleep, see a different city each week, find a new girl wherever ya go, if ya want. Never know if ya leave her with your next baby. You'll never see her again. 'Sides, you're good with the kids and a wrench. It's like ya was born to move, not stay in this armpit town." Ranger tried to convince him. He's got biceps what could ring the High Striker without hittin' the pad's middle, although his voice squeaked like a twelve year old winning the fish bowl game. This one ain't no gazoonie.

"I can't do it. Not wantin' to leave my baby, not for nuthin. Gotta take care of it."

Ain't the last I'll see of him, Ranger knew as the kid turned his back. Next year, he'll be leavin' Rhinebeck. He'd seen dozens like him, and knew a couple more knocks would send this one packin' too.

LOCAL 151
1973, July

"Dad, why the fuck you keep sayin' that? I'm tryin'." And he slammed the door closed as his father watched the olive and rust Pontiac LeMans round the corner, its heft slanting it nearly 15 degrees with the velocity Jake forced into it.

Thoughts ricocheted like pool balls he couldn't control. Jake pointed the hood towards the railroad tracks that parallel the river, a place he and Ka used to come to get high and fool around, in whatever order they felt. He parked the LeMans in a stand of trees beside the dirt road, walked over the tracks to where Thurgood was conceived about a year ago. Thurgood, that screaming lump back at that house. Thurgood, the name she chose. He couldn't look at the boy without seeing her. And he could see her no more.

Fixin' cars in the winter from Poughkeepsie to Germantown, cleaning up construction sites in the warm weather, washing dishes at Mr. D's Fridays and Saturdays. Each shitty job paid his gas and got his alcohol until his alcohol lost him the shitty jobs. At least his father hadn't kicked him out, even though it'd been a year since quittin' school.

His bosses at the garages they told him how naturally he worked with tools and seemed to understand cars. How he worked competently, quietly and never complained about shit jobs like cleaning toilets or stacking tires. How wrenches in his hands moved smoothly, never stripping or over tensioning parts, like a paintbrush to Picasso one even said. At least before lunch.

After vodka filled breaks his work plummeted. Repairs remained excellent, coaxing even the tightest jobs into place with perfection, but he snapped at customers and coworkers. His bosses fired him, afraid of the loss of business and fights among mechanics, or so they said.

Screw them. He threw an empty bottle forty feet into the river, twirling towards its freedom, splashing; the current carried it away from the shitty armpit town.

FEEDING THE LIONESS
1987, June

The Friday morning after school closed Drew, Chris and Steele gathered with their camping gear. Their packs had been stifled with outdated books, ratty notebooks, broken pencils, and rank gym clothes for nearly ten months. This day the backpacks felt more comfortable, more useful, more alive.

Steele told them the hiking plan he blurted out to Papa, about skirting past Millerd's Pond to go camping in the woods nearby. Chris and Drew traded worried looks.

When explaining the adventure to his parents Drew told them, "we'll walk through the Haakinson orchard and up the hill at the north side of the trees then camp in the trees on top of the hill then they asked for your numbers and I gave them your numbers because they said they wanted that in case of an emergency, parents always think someone's going to die probably one of them because they're so old and we will be back on Sunday evening." His parents also insisted on carrying sunscreen, he and his redheaded family with their fair skin fry in direct sun, not unlike vampires.

Chris explained to his family that they would finish at Drew's house on Saturday after two days and a night camping out just beyond the cornfield. He also left phone numbers with his parents, "in case something happens."

Steele glanced at his plastic transparent watch, styled to see the mechanics behind the watch face. If it had been seven days earlier they would be late for their third period class, eighth grade English, with Ms. Getty—or Baffling Betty, as students snickered her name.

Steele had memorized her lore better than most of her lessons. She started in 1957 at Red Hook Central High School as an English teacher, floating between high school and middle school like a leaf caught in an updraft. Rumors circulated she owned upwards of two hundred pairs of shoes, each pair matching identically in color with a pleated skirt, chiffon scarf, and blouse. Each pair a size 7 ½, each pair purchased around 1959.

In one school year she would not repeat an outfit. Over two decades one or two students each year took it upon themselves to record her specific outfit including outstanding features, such as floral print or polka-dots. Steele volunteered for the 1986-87 round as a way to keep his attention. And, in a nerdy way, he enjoyed studying the details and how the patterns repeated year to year. The color sequence, from first day of class just after Labor Day to the last day of finals after Memorial Day, completed its annual pattern. Steele confirmed this with the 1985-86 records. The progression began in pinks and reds, melded to oranges and yellows, lingered in greens through the winter, and burst into blues with spring, closing out in purples by June. Betty travelled the rainbow.

By the mid 80s when she stood at the front of the classroom her hair seemed solid gray from the back row. As she approached a student's desk the contrast between black and white emerged. She piled it in curls meticulously each day, as if each strand were placed on her head every morning and removed before going to sleep.

Clothes and hair distracted students from amazingly drab grammar lessons that droned for ages, even the most studious pupils drifting into daydreams.

Unless the Tigress summoned.

While explaining an archaic grammar rule, such as proper

uses of a seldom-used punctuation mark or the future perfect continuous negative verb tense, her body froze when the Tigress called. She focused on the ring on the middle finger of her right hand, as if answering a telephone. With her left thumb behind her right ring finger, and the other fingers spread as if antennae, she stared blankly at her hands mumbling mysterious instructions, such as feeding the Tigress after lunch and if that wasn't good enough then to find another mistress.

After a few seconds of conversing with her ring, its elongated oval Nephrite jade set in glimmering silver, she continued the instructional sentence exactly where she stopped without the slightest hesitation or realization of her mystifying conversations. At that point no student cared about the lesson, and the lunchroom buzzed with whispers of the Tigress's latest message.

Betty's house popped like a gaudy aunt at a family holiday party. The boys arrived at the front of Betty's house the morning of *That Night*, everything about it remained still, even the leaves of the trees unmoving with the early breeze. It stood steeped in pink, 1950's Cadillac pink, pepto pink, and although grotesquely bright it dully contrasted with the canary yellow of the shutters, door, and porch. A stately Victorian house well over one hundred years old, standing beside several others, with a steeply angled roof and rounded turret, it guarded the entrance to the woods. A porch with several wide steps housing a swing and Adirondack chairs beneath years of grime, awaiting afternoon chats for no visitors. The laziness of pampered youth compelled the boys to brave the shortcut through her yard to cut off a couple miles of the hike to the fiddler.

The boys clambered through a split rail fence. Betty hadn't attacked it in over a decade with her paint brushes, and its grayed, weathered surface offered splinters to passing children.

As they crept along the shin-length lawn they left a noticeable wake, their path a slightly rustled stream of lighter growth flowing through the weeds dotted with groups of dandelions, some reaching the height of their knees, shining yellow in the strengthening morning light.

They cautiously approached the side of the still house where forgotten ladders and piles of jagged rocks sat encased in untended marigolds. Around back Steele motioned towards the bony beagle tied at the far end of the yard, its ribs clinging to bones as if it hadn't seen food since midterms. Drew reached out to grab Chris's arm in warning, and Chris shoved Drew's hand away like an empty Cheezey Oodles bag.

Steele hushed them both when the starving dog detected the boys by moving its ears to better listen. It slowly rose, tottered over to another patch of trodden dirt and circled three quarters, making a sluggish inspection. After presumably deciding the latter dirt was more comfortable than the former dirt it plopped down and sighed wearily. To get to the trailhead they passed within five feet of the weak log with legs.

TEMPORAL STREAMS
1987, June

Around noon, as heat thickened and stomachs growled, the friends paused beside a weakening stream, its thick mud a reminder of its wider path. Beyond the other side of rocks, now out of the boys' sight, another yearlong stream continued unphased by cold or hot; wet or dry. Papa showed Steele this precise spot, Steele remembered when coming upon it with Drew and Chris. He and Papa perched in the outcrop between streams around this time of year, overlooking the disappearing stream on one side and the stream continuously flowing one the other side.

Two months earlier it had reached its peak flow, carrying melted snow and spring rains towards the Hudson River and Atlantic Ocean beyond. By August it would dry to hardened soil. In autumn the dry streambed would host leaves of browns and reds, yellows, oranges; a small meandering trail surrounded on either side by jagged rocks and trees preparing for the oncoming snow. Cycle of life and death, Papa called it.

With the steady stream to their right and the trickle to the left Papa asked Steele what he heard. The young boy answered, "I hear the birds, wind, and water, I guess."

"I *hear* birds singing, wind in the leaves and the fall of water over those rocks," Papa pointed downstream to their right about ten yards. "But when I *listen* I notice what is truly around me. I come to this spot to learn. Many years ago, when Grandma Lilli transitioned to her new phase of existence, I came here. The wind rustling the leaves told me to continue on, to push around the obstacles in my path. Seeing the leaves turned over, but clinging to their branches, showed me that although my life felt upside down, persistence would be crucial for my life to continue. Grandma's passing was a gust of wind, and like a leaf I stayed with my branch for its nourishment and to nourish it.

"I looked at this seasonal stream," he pointed to the left, "and the other. Grandma was the one that flows in spring. She left a path in her wake, a bed to be remembered by. She's not forgotten. Even as the water disappears it continues to exist, intent to join this other stream, the one with water flowing year round."

The young Steele gazed down where the two streams merged, wondering if Grandma Lilli was buried there. Papa had mentioned she rested out here, somewhere.

Papa went on. "I saw myself as this stream, flowing in the same direction, side by side with the seasonal stream. The streams connect at the junction before the small waterfall. Their unity cannot be broken. I will continue as this stream that flows year round. The water in the stream moves as my spirit moves in me. My body is the streambed, providing the path to hold my spirit. Grandma Lilli's spirit flowed down the river, to a bigger streambed with more water, having outgrown her body. Just as I will move on. Someday." The boy and man stared at the water dropping from the rocks; a constant muzzled bubbling filling their ears.

"What about the birds?" Steele, enjoying their harmoniously chaotic songs.

"The birds exist to sing," Papa answered simply and lapsed into silence.

A makeshift bridge over the stream's narrowest part led the boys to the outcropping. A fallen tree disintegrated to a pulpy sponge. Odd planks completed the bridge, carrying a surefooted person across without a drop of water touching their toes.

Steele didn't mention any of Papa's streambed or leaf philosophy to Chris or Drew as they ate peanut butter and jelly sandwiches on the ridge. Chris mentioned he'd been there before, and knew the way towards the cabin. Follow the stream. Past the swamp, until Mill Road.

Steele asked, curious, "How do we get around the swamp and stream?"

"I don't know. I guess we'll find a way," Chris shrugged. He usually found a way to get what he wanted, such as the time he brought an English Bulldog home and told his parents a concocted story about it being a stray; in truth he freed it from a house about two miles away.

"Guys, I'm starting to think this is a big mistake I don't think we should go through the swamp or to the road we should go home," Drew blurted to the rocks between his feet.

"Go home if you want, wussy" Chris spat with disdain, "I'm finding Fiddler's Bridge and I'm gonna listen to the fiddler play if it's true. I'm not going back."

"I just don't think it's right going so far from home without our parents knowing where we are or what we're doin' I've never done anything like this before and..." Drew trailed off.

"If you're scared, go home, Drew. I don't want a jerk like you to keep us back. Go!"

"Don't call me a jerk, you bastard."

"Fuck you!" Drew flicked his middle finger at Chris.

"No, fuck you and your hot mom!" Chris stood up. Drew leaped in response, dropping his sandwich crusts to the ground.

Steele pierced the argument. "Listen, Drew, you don't have to come. Chris and I want to see if there's really a ghost near that bridge. You're coming to try and be cool. We know that. Not because you really want to. Choose now—do you want to go to Fiddler's Bridge or just go home?"

Drew looked dazed, as if Steele just whacked him on the head with a baseball bat. To do something you didn't want to do, just to be cool for the other kids was as common as Mr. D's pizza on Friday night. But to be called out on it was the biggest smack of reality a thirteen year old could have. Drew grabbed his backpack and stomped out of sight.

He stopped about ten feet from them, fished around in his backpack and pulled out a can of mosquito repellant, cocked his arm back, and flung the can into the running stream so Chris and Steele wouldn't have any bug spray. He glanced Steele's direction with a half smile on his face and resumed his retreat.

Chris shrugged and admitted, "I'm glad he's gone. He's been pissing me off since we left this morning. Even before that."

"Yeah, but I hope he cools down before he gets home. I don't want him telling on us. I'll be in deep shit if Papa finds out what I'm up to."

"Don't worry about it. Let's go."

They brushed off their shorts, fashionably designed for beaches 3,000 miles away rather than hiking dense New York woods.

As they navigated towards the swamp they each selected walking sticks to steady their balance. A mixture of marsh, standing lime-green algae-covered water, trees, and occasional patches of land spanned the swamp. It stretched forward out of sight and to either side. They knew from the older kids that there was a way to move across it without getting wet. Neither had ever done it before, and Steele knew that little fact wouldn't stop Chris from leading the charge.

They dodged roots, ducked under branches, hopped on fallen trees and grassy knolls, crossing the murky waters still dry. Another stream flowed out of the swamp, and where the stream started and swamp ended rested a shallow pool no more that one foot deep at its lowest point, about ten yards across with rocks at odd intervals. The last rock protruded above the surface eight feet from the far edge of the swamp. They paused to survey the options.

Chris clutched his stick as a tightrope walker would and took one final leap from the last stone. Steele doubted Chris would make it all the way. He landed as if he had flown with the sandals of Mercury, wings clipped. Without a second thought about where he splashed down he sloshed the remainder of the shallow pool to the other side, waving his arm above his head and shouted, "C'mon in, man, the water's great."

DUTYRONOMY
1972, April

Between first and second periods they jumped into Jake's LeMans heading to the river just south of Tivoli. She brought the grass and he took a bottle of vodka from his father's liquor cabinet with the faulty lock as the first warm April day ignited their hormones in symbiotic ecstasy. Indulging first in the back seat, second in the wagon's bed, and finally at the river's high tide edge they climaxed and climaxed again until exhaustion knocked them unconscious.

A trolling fisherman's motor humming twenty feet out in the river woke Marika. Head still dizzy and tingling between her legs, she wondered what time it was. "Jake, wake up," she nudged his shoulder, and when that didn't work she fondled him, "I need to get back to school."

"I ain't goin' to that hell hole," he mumbled groggily. "This is heaven, Ka, why leave it? We've got the river, the trees with new leaves, the wind, a bottle of booze. I don't need no school. Teachers are assholes."

"I don't want my parents to know. They'll freak out."

"Your parents can fuck themselves," he traced his finger over the birthmark on her bicep, her fairy tale hair splaying as if a frozen waterfall.

"Don't say…" she started off as a train drowned her out. He

hardened once more and after another volley he agreed to take her back to school, leaving permanent rubber reminders of temporary thrills scattered among the wildflowers.

"Jake, where do you want to go? This place is too small, nothing's happening here. We can't stay. San Francisco? The city?"

"I ain't goin' nowhere. I don't like it here, but I gotta stay for my old man. What the hell would we do? I ain't protesting no goddamn war. Killin' commies needs to be done. I'd shoot one now if they was here, right between them squinty eyes, Ka."

"No, you need to respect life. There's no reason to kill or hurt another person, Jake." The top of the hill approached beyond the dented hood, the last summit before descending to town.

"Ka, y'know I love you."

She couldn't say it back. Not today. Not again.

Jake dropped her off one block from the school, between the Catholic school and the priest's house. A distant bell ended a class period. Jake thought of that crazy English teacher with her Tigress and green ring and wacked up eyes that changed between green and black, and how Ka screwed around keeping track of the color of her dresses all year.

Jake rounded the next corner to the right as Marika watched. The LeMans's mass listed port side, barely missing the car in the next lane, Jake oblivious to his father in the driver's seat.

SUMMER, HIGH
1972, July

Oregano and garlic flavored air soothed Marika at Mr. D's, the first pizza restaurant to creep into Red Hook, where Jake remained after closing. "They all went for the fireworks, left the bar open." He poured several shots in a glass, flavoring it with cola, and mixed a second, smaller drink for her.

"Jake, you need to come back to school in fall. You're not going to get better jobs without a diploma."

"I ain't goin' back to school. That shit hole's seen the last of me. I'm makin' money now, ain't no one gonna pay me to sit there learnin'. 'Sides, I'm savin' up for us. For our move to Boulder. I don't learn so good with books. Gimme a hammer, I'll build you a house. Gimme a book, I'll build you a fire." Marika shrank back, a tiny, ornate pipe with Gaelic etchings materializing from her bag.

Reclining in the back of the LeMans, its tailgate open, Marika's mind opened up after one hit. Boulder. High in Colorado. The corners of her mouth curled, the apples of her cheekbones flushed from the pun and the enlightening fog swirled her thoughts. Joining her spirit with others working for peace and universal love, showing the world the possibilities of prizing each other over material possessions. Turn off the TV, tune into nature, turn back political tumult and turbidity, two

hundred tulips blazing fiercely over late winter snow, twenty....
"Have another hit," Jake interrupted her muddled flow with his
clenched breath, he exhaled, and dandled her dress loose.

Marika gazed out the LeMans without sharing news of life
growing in her, final ripples of orgasms still fresh, dreams of
Boulder brightening the pot's shadows. She couldn't hide it from
him much longer, already slightly bulging.

She'd been gardening that summer learning to grow zucchini,
squashes, tomatoes, cucumbers, and beans. Taking manure from
a neighbor's cows she'd experimented with small batches of
compost tea for the vegetables, noticing their magnified growth
from extra nutrients. Her mind wandered to lovely recipes and
wondering how to can tomatoes—she had seen her grandmother
with glass jars and large steaming pots and would learn with her.
Thoughts of the succulent red flesh, soothing and cool despite
hot summer sun, started her stomach panging; hunger brusquely
called her back to the restaurants' parking lot.

The night's sticky humidity clung around the lovers like mold
on melons as fireworks popped and fizzed. As they lay their
sudor mingled with sweat from the oppressive night. He clamped
down the peace abruptly, "Ka, you pregnant, or what?"

Her hand instinctively rubbed her abdomen.

"You gonna get rid of it, right?"

Silence.

Her fingertips traced deliberate, tiny circles below her navel.

"I don't want no kid, I ain't even eighteen yet. You ain't
neither. You gotta take it out. There's a place near—".

"No," she cut him off. She knew he wouldn't want to keep it.
He callously cared only for himself. "It's mine. All life is
precious. And this life is mine." And yours, she thought, with
doubt suppressed below her conscious horizon.

"It's legal now in New York. I ain't takin' care of no kid."

This child will be born, she decided. If Jake won't help, she'd
raise it by herself. In Boulder.

TIGRESS'S MESSAGE
1972, October

By apple season her belly left no doubts. Her teachers, with the exception of Baffling Betty, ignored her outside of routine roll call. Even though Betty no longer taught Marika, she stopped the pregnant girl in the church's parking lot, inserting herself between Marika and Jacob. Betty peered into Marika's eyes with her jade green, luminescent irises tinged with black specks. Marika, not wanting to bring more attention to her by being seen with the unpredictable instructor, fidgeted to leave.

"This boy you're carrying, his future cannot be read. The Tigress whispers opaquely," she spread her fingers over Marika's stomach like a bowling ball. "His father, whether in flesh or forgotten, will shadow him." Her head snapped back, the ring rested on Marika's belly quivering slightly, "Tigress mumbles...lineage muddied...Tigress sees misgivings...mistakes yet unmade...stream of regrets...healing...past is future."

Marika backed away, ready to leave this crazy woman, the teacher's hand separating from her growing womb. Marika caught Betty's eyes once more, eyes now moonless midnight black. "Have a lovely afternoon, dear. I hope to see you at the Poetry Club soon."

"She's higher than the moon," Jake scowled as Betty pranced away.

Marika's isolation reemerged, fiercer than ever. Friends abandoned her when learning of the gentle life growing inside of her; her parents barely tolerated her in their house, barking only the basic commands at her, never more than four words at a time. "Get up!" "Time to eat." "Get out." "Go to school."

An aura of disquiet clouded the reality of autumn briskness and vibrant leaves. The sidewalk and the brick-faced buildings circulated around her, intangible and shadowed in deep purples. She'd only sensed this once before, at the death of her younger brother after diving into a neighbor's pool four years earlier. Unless Jake would take classes, she'd have no place to go. Perhaps she could sell some pot, or other favors, to muster bus fare out west.

CULTIVATED VARIETIES
1972, October

The town's festival drew crowds from as far as New York City and Hartford. From Hardscrabble Plaza on South Broadway, rounding the corner at Market Street where the judges' platform rose above the crowd, and west to the edge of downtown at the field separating the junior high from the high school, Red Delicious floats floated; the Grannies Smith marchers marched in step; Yellow Delicious bands bandied their tunes; and hopefuls for the crown of McIntosh Queen glimmered in garnet red dresses waved aspiringly to onlookers.

Levi Steele founded and chaired the Red Hook Apple Festival and Parade Foundation, served as lead judge for the parade and the deciding voter for the McIntosh Queen pageant. Other than the Red Hook Apple Festival and Parade, the town raised no boasting point—no Bunyan-sized ball of yarn spun from townspeople's hair; not an entrepreneurial museum dedicated to shoelaces or shrikes, shovels or short division; not even a room where George Washington once slept.

This year's featured apple, selected by Levi, promoted the Winesap. Noticing a decline in its popularity in the last decade, he chose it for its deep, nearly scarlet skin and simple sweet flavors. Biting into a Winesap, Levi enjoyed its delicate skin balanced by crisp, firm interior with slight notes of honey. His grandfather used Winesap, or Wine Sop as known then, as the primary base for cider. Levi hoped the cider competition would feature at least a couple dominant Winesap tastings.

The Fortune had been a close contender, its firm flesh with a zesty bite versatile from fresh eating to cooking. The variations in color—specks of green and yellow flecking the dominant red—likened it visually to a McIntosh or Empire, and the Fortune's name projected a strong future. With the Paula Red's early peak harvest passing two weeks prior Levi knocked that out of contention. Nostalgia—and the hope for some unique cider—pushed Levi to the Winesap.

Levi inspected the scaffolding of the judges' stand as Jacob approached him holding Marika's hand.

"Hi, Mr. Steele." Marika forced a smile, eyes looking down, her blond hair falling nearly to her enlarged buttocks.

Levi admired the shape of her pregnancy. "He's protruding like a Cortland." Sensing that the analogy was lost on Marika, he continued, "Cortland apples are squat and flatter than most varieties, pushing out wide to the sides. Only boys grow like Cortlands. If you were narrow and slim, more of a vertical shape like a Glockenapfel, I'd guess it's a girl. Can you feel anything?"

"Yes, sir, mostly at night." Marika instinctively caressed her stomach.

"Excellent. And have your parents come around yet?"

"Dad, they ain't gonna change. Ain't no way the baby's gonna live in their house. Ka and the baby gotta live with us," Jacob answered.

"I've told you that's not happening unless you finish school. If it's Red Hook High School here or going down to BOCES in Poughkeepsie doesn't matter to me.

"And you need to find a job and keep it. That baby will need diapers and clothes. Marika, too, will need food, clothes, and shelter. They'll need a man's support." Confident that the judges' platform was sturdy, Levi started a quick pace south on Broadway towards St. Christopher's Church for the cider tasting stations, paused and commanded, "Come with me."

"Slow down. Ka can't go that fast," Jake reminded his father.

Levi circulated around the tasting tables as Father Seamus drew near, his black hair sprouting new white accents, large glasses engulfing his forehead. Marika and Jacob enjoyed the mulled cider tastings across the church's parking lot. Levi sensed an attack from the priest. "Levi, if your son asks for bread, will you give him a rock? If he asks for an egg, will you give him a scorpion?" The priest's native Irish accent flared with exoticism.

"Father, leave Matthew and Luke out of this. Jacob is my son, I discipline him with kindness." Levi thrilled in their biblical duals, as Jacob and Marika strayed across the parking lot.

"Ah, Proverbs then? True, discipline him while there is hope; but do not will him his death. Do not provoke him to anger," the priest strayed out of Proverbs into Ephesians.

Not to be outquoted by the clergyman, Levi rebutted from Proverbs again. "You may think that I have sired a fool, Father, and this brings me no joy. Jacob is my son and is no fool. Raising a boy without a mother, without Lilli's warmth and discipline, is my cross." Levi jotted notes about a slight lime undertone of the cider from Bringham's Orchard, and flinched as Betty reached towards Marika's stomach out of his earshot.

Levi returned to the debate with the priest. "We can continue our cannon blasts from the old or new testaments all day, our interpretations will not change. Let's agree that we both want Jacob to succeed as a man, we want Marika to raise the child, and we want the child to reach his potential." He lifted two small cups from Ogden Orchard, giving one to the clergyman and toasted, "to fathers and sons."

"Indeed," the priest raised his small paper cup.

"Bold tones of lemon from the top, rosemary and ginger in the finish," Levi observed. No Winesap in this blend.

Across the parking lot Marika shook her head as the crazed teacher dashed away.

EXPANDING VALLEY
1972, November

Two weeks after the apple festival, Jake dropped papers in his father's lap with stubborn finality, BOCES needing signatures to enroll him in a mechanic's program beginning in January, a month before the baby's due date.

"What happens between now and then?" Levi probed.

"Don't know. I'm still scrubbin' pots at Mr. D's. Nothin' else stuck at the garages. I'll ask for more nights."

"Have you thought about regular high school until January? BOCES needs regular classes too."

"I'll get it all at BOCES. You want me to go there or not? Sign them fuckin' papers, then." Jake looked at him with contempt. "Then Ka will come over."

"Not until you start classes. No classes, no Marika in my home." He closed his book, *The Hudson River School: from Beirstadt to Wier.* "She's a lovely girl and needs a stable home now, and I will provide it. We will provide it. I need you to keep your word, and I'll only know that through what I see you do. As Saint—"

Jake cut him off. "I don't need no fuckin' lecture. I ain't no saint. If you wouldn't've sold the farm, maybe I'd have somethin' better to do. All you thought of was yourself, what was best for you and these," stabbing the air all round with a pen, "these damn books. If you'd thought of me, of us, of Grandpa, you'd have figured out how to keep the farm. Now all we've got is this damn house and stories. They ain't gonna provide for me 'n Ka so I've gotta wash fuckin' dishes and fix cars." His face flushed and words finished, he hiked into the woods to smoke a joint. His attack captured more words than he'd spoken to his father since ninth grade, around the time Jake first tapped the liquor cabinet.

It was all for Ka. And the baby. They needed security, and Jake reluctantly swallowed his role in the mess, like crushed aspirin smothered in sugar. She'd refused the abortion and would be on the street—but in this armpit town no one lived on the street, and winters would be deadly. He figured he'd knuckle under and send the papers to BOCES.

***

Levi reflected on the tirade. Jacob's idea of their family wealth emerged from fragments of information dropped along the way, and likely grapevine murmurs from other children around town. Why hadn't he told Jacob the straight truth? What held him back? He's the closest living relative I have, Levi thought, and he's become so distant. Perhaps too far to return.

Regret crept upon Levi, regret the bastard child of sin. Dogmatic teachings of organized religion used pulpit power to influence daily actions and decisions—and when the institutions control your thoughts they control you, he believed. Blindly follow their instructions to be saved. They inundate followers with coded messages. Cross the Word of God (to Levi, the words of gods) and suffer. Suffer from judgment of an unknown, unseeable force—as sin. Believers of these faulty doctrines learned to regret.

Conveniently for the institutions, only the divine's ordained mediators could assuage sin and thus alleviate regret—to create a tree ready to produce more sin, thus sustain the organized religion in perpetuity. Sure, if Levi ate half an apple pie (often known to do so—especially delicately balanced with Granny Smith, Winesap, and Rome Beauty) his stomach might revolt and his mind would be content. By rejecting the teachings and doctrine at the root presumption of sin, he didn't experience regret.

Let Jacob go, Levi decided. He might yet have a decade of self-discovery, a painful trek into the distant abyss of his inner being. Each person's unique journey will be his or hers alone, and though he wished to ease the path's pain for his son, Levi couldn't.

And shouldn't, he knew.

***

Marika longingly expected the slow anticipation of seeing this being, feeding it from her breast, gently stroking its head, hoping it would invoke compassion, love, and attachment. But those feelings eluded her. So far.

Outwardly, at least to Jake and Levi, and to the public clinic's harried nurses, she left that impression. Society impaled traditional norms through the expectant mother's heart—yet Marika's heart suffered a widening distance, a growing gulf between her and the being inside her. Even the thought of it— she couldn't imagine it as a boy or girl, only a genderless thing, a leach sucking her essence, draining her of energy, exacting steep emotional taxes. Just a horrifying nightmare.

Wilma, the pear shaped nurse who evaluated her most often, assured her it seemed to be a routine pregnancy. Marika should feel lucky for no morning sickness. Lucky to have no irregular pains. Gaining weight as expected, luckily not too much and not too little. Lucky to be young. What kind of luck, Marika wondered, to be so young and pregnant?

BLOWN OUT
1973, January

A lucky, smooth birth, the nurse told her as Marika carried the boy to his father's home.

What did Betty tell her that time in the apple festival? Some kind of foggy prediction about mistakes that would come one day. Maybe her mistake was insistence on giving birth to the baby? But Betty (or was it Tigress?) mumbled mistakes not made yet, so perhaps keeping the baby was the right decision. And whose mistakes weren't made yet? Hers? Jake's? Mistakes Thurgood would one day make?

What had Tigress (or Betty) mentioned about wine? Not water to wine, no. Regrets, turning regrets to wine. Had she meant wine, or whine? Turning regrets to whine. Transforming regrets to a mind-altering substance, or a sniveling tone? She briefly wondered whether there were patron saints of wine, whining, or winos. Levi would know, but she would never ask him. Whose regrets, and which regrets? Tigress/Betty shrouded the prediction.

Holding him, Marika's emotional chasm intensified. Her passion for all living beings did not extend to Thurgood, her child. Marked at birth with a strip shaped like Florida on his right upper arm, likely to darken with age just as hers had. A glimpse of his vacant green eyes elicited nothing within her. Not love, not contempt, no variations of the spectrum of emotional connections, just lack. She nursed him and nourishment flowed abundantly, yet the vacuum of her feelings repelled her from this act, turning her to formula feeding. At least Jake—and occasionally Levi—could feed him that way, lessening her physical time burdened by him.

An early March blizzard erased all it touched. A gentle swell in the driveway hinted at the LeMans below, but driveway and street and yard merged as one great whiteness. Marika vanished with the storm, leaving a wax sealed letter for the boy.

The next county fair blew into town that summer and swept Jake away with it, leaving the infant latched to Levi.

SINKING BURIAL
2000 Three

Distant whispers beneath ground crept into his mind, an eldritch tingling inching up his spine. Laying supine, trees towered above, swaying fiercely; budding, greening, yellowing, dropping, burying him; the annual cycle accelerating and simultaneously ghastly still. Cold, invisible iron claws pinned his limbs. Icy sweat. Futile struggles. Surrender, the only option. Come death, come drowning. Welcome the end. Whispers equal sensations—cipher coded in pulses and vibrations. Meaning? No meaning. A key. Not meant for him. Body slips, seduced into darkness; warmth below the surface; comfort darker than six moonless midnights, submerged within viscous undersoil; merged in whispers, voiceless rustle prickling his skin. Naked, shivering despite the heat; his spine trickles. Blood? Mud? No pain. Grief grips his abdomen.

Drew wakened.

The dream.

Again.

PASSING
February 2000

A decade earlier grunge rock hit the banks of the Hudson in this exhausted bar, serving under age kids thrashing to local fad bands Spanky Noodle and Pulsing Brow. Spankings over and the pulse gone flat, local stragglers creep in for a draught and a memory at the bedraggled Victorian counter, with occasional escapees from the city soaking in nearly a century and a half of imagined fights, undecipherable lyrics, harlots. One of Steele's feet grounded him in the local scene, and for more than half a decade his studies and research flung him to Manhattan. When Papa's MedAlertLine interrupted his class, he bolted to Grand Central Station for the next Metro-North to Poughkeepsie. The department chair assured him she would cover the classes as long as needed, as she also specialized in Mid-Atlantic and New England pre-colonial history.

"Up there are your mother's belongings, and toys," Papa inched his trembling hand towards the ceiling, "in the attic." He paused to take a breath from the exertion of the movement, "but do me a favor, go up only when I'm gone."

Steele impulsively shook his head in denial.

"Don't fight it, Thurgood, I'm transitioning to the next phase of my journey." Protesting or rebuttals being pointless efforts with Papa, Steele nodded. "Joining Lilli in her stream."

"And your books, what do you want with them?" thinking of his research, or at least benefit the Red Hook and Rhinebeck libraries.

"Thurgood, don't fret. Jacob walked out of our lives almost thirty years ago. The lawyer in Roundout has the will." He wheezed from under the brown and orange crocheted blanket.

FIDDLER'S BRIDGE
1987, June

"No way we'll get there today, not through the woods." Without Drew's directions, they couldn't find a flea on a mangy dog's ass, let alone Fiddler's Bridge. "So, what to do?" Chris peered through the trees perhaps hoping a guiding star might appear in mid-afternoon.

Go home, Steele thought. "What do you want to do?"

"You have no fuckin' ideas, Steele?"

"I have ideas." Like give this up, go swimming, listen to R.E.M.'s Reckoning. "Let's walk towards the golf course, follow the edge to the road, see if we can get a ride at least to Milan. DelVecchio's oldest brother works there in the summer, maybe he can drop us closer."

The abandoned Corvette rested where they heard it would be: 100 yards away from the airstrip near the golf course; trees so thick surrounding it that the shell seemingly grew out of the ground. The carcass, picked over by hundreds of curious teens before them, left the two boys' half hearted attempts to scavenge anything from the wreck fruitless. Decaying leaves flowed from the open trunk, a rogue apple tree popped from the hood, untended life sprouting from forgotten histories. They moved on, closer to the golf course.

Near a fairway, twenty feet beyond the tree line, Chris spotted his father. "Dammit, quiet Steele. If we're caught now I'll be whipped. Probably right here too. He thinks we're just beyond the cornfield near the neighborhood. Damn." The foursome, two men and two women, played through. His father coached one of the women through a swing, holding her from behind, adjusting her grip on the club, lingering much longer than necessary, finishing with a tap on her rear.

"Did you see how he treated that lady?"

"Who is she?"

"Someone from work, I think. Bastard." Drew grunted defiantly.

"Don't worry about it. Let's find Troy," Steele said, wishing to distract Chris from his father's flirting.

At the equipment building Troy just returned from mowing near the roadway, finishing his day. He agreed to bring them towards Milan. "Shotgun!" Chris sprinted to the car claiming the front seat. Settling in, he asked about the lady with his father.

"Yeah, I see them twice a week, Tuesdays and Fridays. Usually with that other couple, but sometimes just the two of them. Why?" Troy pointed the car south, soon turning left. He smelled like fresh cut grass and sweat, so Chris and Steele cranked down their windows.

"He tells us he's in Albany Tuesdays and Fridays, for meetings. Bastard is lying to us." Chris folded his arms with fists clenched and lapsed into a furious silence.

Steele told Troy their plans.

"It's all bullshit, you know. I've gone there one night didn't hear anything. Stayed for hours. Mosquitos are a bitch," Troy replied, starting down the empty road.

"Were you there during a waning moon?"

"I don't remember. I didn't see the moon. It was cloudy. Still, everyone I've talked with that's been out there never heard the fiddler. It's bullshit."

"Well, we're gonna try anyhow," Steele insisted.

Chris remained violently silent.

"Ever hear of the haunting at the Rhinecliff Hotel?" Troy

looked in the rearview mirror to see Steele.

Steele shook his head.

"Alright. So, it's not at the hotel itself, but in the train station just next to it. No bull. I've seen this one, fucking creepy.

"So, the hotel started as a stopover for travelers on horseback; but soon the train also came through from the city to Albany. Apparently just after the Civil War one evening the train stopped and a few politicians on their way to Albany got out for a quick drink, stayed too long and missed the train.

"The next train was in the morning, so they kept drinking. A local businessman, one of those rich guys looking for a spot to build a huge house overlooking the river, also sat drinking. He recognized one of the politicians, who thought the businessman was a Congressman from the city. They started talking bullshit politics and bullshit business, since this local guy made cement near Rosendale. He wanted a Reconstruction contract. He'd also had some bullshit investments in cotton mills in the South, and the end of slavery slammed his businesses there." Troy turned right down Milan Hollow Road, Chris's fists still knotted.

"They started arguing some bullshit and headed outside, towards the tracks. People heard shouting, then a couple shots rang out," Troy paused, "can you guess the rest?"

"One of the guys died, and his ghost can be seen sometimes around the hotel," Steele ventured.

"Nope. The guys were too drunk to fire straight. They killed a horse. Belonged to the local businessman."

"So, is there a ghost now?"

"Some people say they see a horse standing near the tracks. I've seen it. You believe that horseshit?" At least he didn't say bullshit again, Steele thought. They continued down the road, soon turning at Bull's Head Road.

Animal ghosts, why not? "I've never heard of a horse ghost, but I guess it could happen," Steele shrugged.

"If there are spirits of people, why not animals? What might the horse still need from this world?" Troy caught Steele's eyes in the mirror taking it further. "The headless horseman rides a horse, right? So is that horse a ghost, right? And that's halfway to the city, not too far. So, sure, animals can have ghosts."

"Maybe the Rhinecliff ghost horse needs to make a delivery?" Steele guessed.

The car jolted right, missing a pickup from the other direction by inches. Troy slammed the brakes and the pickup jolted to a stop, the driver huffed to Troy's door, bending over to expose a plumber's crack that could swallow a deck of cards.

With silent communication evolved from years of friendship between Steele and Chris, after an instant eye check and slight head nod they agreed to duck out of the car and walk, grabbing their backpacks. The barrel barking at Troy sounded angry, but they heard laughter once the boys turned left on Center Road, "Well, ain't that just the shit!" the rotund guy bellowed.

Chris unclenched his hands, but his vein traced like lightning bolts beside his temple.

Not another car passed as they walked south towards the bridge, still a couple miles to go, Chris's thick cloak of rage hovering between them. Chris angrily grabbed rocks, fiercely chucking them deep in the woods at no particular target while hoping for maximum damage. He whacked at weeds, slapped flowers, spit on tree branches, and flicked sticks. Everything in their path felt his wrath.

Steele's mind skipped to the ghost horse of Rhinecliff. Did it have a saddle? What color was it, what breed? Would it walk near the tracks, would it neigh? And what happened to the businessman and politician? If the horse's spirit could be seen, would it be translucent or solid? Maybe Troy had more details to share if he hadn't nearly sideswiped the pickup. Papa likely knew the story, Steele decided to ask him later.

Steele yearned to hear the fiddler's tunes that night. It could be true, or a story embellished for centuries. Papa never mentioned anyone actually seeing the fiddler, only hearing his music. What did music of that era sound like? How much did fiddle music change with time? Would they hear an entire song, or just crumbs? And even if they heard it, would his life tomorrow be any different than life today?

The ethereal echo snuck into Steele's mind again, the same whispering voice he heard that morning, eerily familiar yet foreign too. *TURN BACK. YOUR FRIEND MUST NOT CONTINUE.* His stomach sank, dense and nauseous; just as when it first murmured across ages to him.

He deliberated. Maybe they should turn back. But Chris's stubbornness drove him when he decided to take on the challenge, and Steele would not abandon his friend. Papa instilled loyalty in him. He ignored the voice—how could he be hearing voices in his own head anyhow?

Chris froze as if at the edge of a cliff. Screamed. "THAT FUCKER. LYING, CHEATING, FUCKER! FUCK HIM!" Fists clenched. Scarlett cheeks.

"Let's take a break, go sit on the boulders over there," Steele pointed about thirty feet inside the tree line. Not waiting for Chris's reaction he blazed the path.

Chris smashed a bracket fungus as long as a football from a decaying log, dropkicked an imaginary field goal with it and collapsed on the rocks. "For three years he's gone to these meetings in Albany. So, if he's golfing in the summer, what's going on in the winter?" Chris idolized his father, focused on becoming a computer scientist at IBM just like him.

"Glad Troy gave us the ride. Want some Cheezey Oodles?" Steele thought of no other response for Chris.

Chris ignored Steele and returned to the road thrashing undergrowth in his way.

After forty minutes in silence Chris asked, "Where's the fuckin' bridge?"

"I dunno, let's just walk that way," Steele pointed left, "we'll find it."

In Steele's imagination he pictured a deep gulley of jagged rocks and exposed tree roots surrounding a quick flowing creek. The reality—when they found the place most likely to be Fiddler's Bridge—disappointed big time. A gradual slope led to a wide, lazy stream. The waters trickled out from a cow field towards a dense stand of trees and shrubs on the opposite side of the road with a steel deck bridge sporting no safety railings. Unless walking it would be barely noticeable. "Is this it?" Steele hoped not.

Chris shrugged.

"Not what I thought it would be. Maybe back when the fiddler died it was deeper? Before they paved the road?" Steele speculated.

"As far as I know, there's only one bridge on this road. Maybe two. This is the biggest one."

"So now what?"

"We wait. Let's find a place in the trees for the tents." Chris scanned the area for a campsite.

While setting up his tent Steele noticed Chris laying his on top of gnarled surface roots. Even with a foam pad (which neither boy brought) his back would knot—on top of maybe, perhaps, hearing a ghost's music and stewing over his father's affair this could not be a restful night. Steele showed Chris a better site and started unfurling his own shelter when Chris asked almost inaudibly, "Steele, what do you know about your father?"

Steele never talked much about that. But since the topic might cool Chris's temper about his father, Steele opened.

"Papa has never told me much, y'know. I picked up bits and pieces along the way. Apparently Jacob cherished a 1966 Pontiac LeMans more than anything or anyone. He knew how to fix it and lots of other stuff—cars, tractors, fridges, washers, dryers— pretty much any machine." Papa insisted to Steele that since Jacob left when he was an infant he shouldn't refer to Jacob as his father. "Jacob never finished high school, took off when he would've been in eleventh grade, I think. Papa said he became a carny, going from fair to fair setting up rides and games and stuff."

"That's all?"

"Well, Papa told me some stories. Told me once about why he thinks Jacob left. But it's a long story."

"We've got a lot of time until the moon's up. Nothin' else to do." Chris seemed slightly relaxed, the veins along his temples receded, closer to normal. He opened a bag of Cheezey Oodles.

"Yup. Okay." Steele dug to recall all the details, though some escaped. "Apparently back in the day Papa's family owned lots of land around town. Hundreds of acres. They grew apples, operated a dairy. Some of the land was too hilly to farm so it stayed woods. When Papa inherited the land he sold some cheaply, or donated it, I'm not sure, so they could build the high school."

Chris nodded; most people knew that about Steele's family. Steele's poles assembled, he looked for stakes in the bag, only finding two.

"Jacob didn't like school, skipped most days and eventually dropped out. He worked some odd jobs like washing dishes at Mr. D's and repairing cars at a few garages. I guess he couldn't keep any of the jobs long, except the dishwashing. Papa said Jacob used to smoke a lot of pot, steal alcohol, and stay out a lot of nights."

"Sounds like your opposite," Chris joked.

"Um hmm," Steele murmured, "total loser. Papa said that the only time of year Jacob enjoyed was the Dutchess County Fair. He used to go over there and take a job with the carnies, did that for a few years in a row." R.E.M.'s Carnival of Sorts (Boxcars) popped into his head with Bill Berry's pounding drums accelerating the wandering stranger's journey through the song.

"You ever hear from him?" Chris's tent completed, he helped Steele tie up the complicated A-frame's external poles.

"Nope. Never. I've seen a couple pictures from his yearbooks. We look a lot alike, when he was about my age. Papa said Jacob wasn't happy with the situation—a baby, no reliable job, still just a teenager himself. He thinks Jacob needed to discover who he was, not who he had become. I think Papa still hopes, deep down, that Jacob will come back one day. Not to raise me, but just to know that he's still alive."

"What do you think about him leaving you when you were a baby?"

"I dunno. I get angry sometimes. I wonder what it might've

been like to grow up with him around. I might've learned how to fix things, build stuff, work on cars. Papa's shown me some of that, but he's older and can't do as much as he could fifteen or twenty years ago. Sometimes I'm jealous when I see you and Drew with your dads."

Chris's face knotted like the root near his tent, his eyes shooting daggers.

"You know what I mean, before today."

Chris's rage at his father blew like a firecracker, while Steele's feelings towards Jacob simmered like a witch's brew. Steele wondered every day what life might have been if both his parents raised him. He knew even less about his mother. He read her name from his birth certificate, and her parents moved away a couple years after he was born. Maybe Jacob would have owned a garage, Steele could have worked there over summers and weekends. Maybe his mother would have cooked like a Culinary Institute of America chef, or maybe she burned spaghetti. Steele would never know how her food tasted. Never know the sound of her voice, shrill or flat or gravelly or quiet. Maybe she'd have been a lawyer, a real estate agent, a secretary, or an IBMer. What would make Jacob or Marika angry enough to hit him—or even if they would believe in physical punishment? Would they drink too much, still smoke pot? What would make them laugh? How could he make them proud? He'd never know any of the answers, yet he carried his leaded yoke moment to moment; this unresolved weight their legacy.

The pull of discovery distracted the boys—the thrill of finding new wild places; trees and ground and waters in combinations they'd never seen, wondering who walked these grounds before them—Indians or Dutch, British or Americans. Steele would feel lucky if they crossed some forgotten remnant of past people like low, slate walls. They hiked beside the creek away from the road, each tossing in a small stick to race downstream, carrying a longer branch to dislodge the tiny boat when it jammed along the way; a game they had played since third grade.

Returning to camp after a couple hours they found the tents

crumbled, poles thrown all around. "WHAT THE F—," Chris started.

"Well, ain't that just the shit," a voice shouted from the road, "you them same two boys in that car that nearly slammed my truck." The barrel shaped guy from earlier toddled towards them through the brush. "This is private land, boys. I'll give you two minutes to get your crap out, or I'll be calling the cops for trespassin'." His rifle put an exclamation point on his threat. "If you think you'll hear the ghost tonight, you're outta luck. There ain't no ghost, no fiddler, nothin but that crick. 'Sides, folks say he only plays after Halloween. I ain't never heard him, don't believe in that crap." Steele's stomach and hearted pounded, the first time a gun pointed his general direction. They scrambled with the gear and the guy went on jabbering. "That boy's funny, your friend in the car, but this ain't no joke climbin' on someone else's land. You boys ain't the first ones been out here, ain't gonna be the last ones neither." His eyes stuck to Steele, as if struggling to recall a name of a movie actor popular in 1972.

Recognition dawned on him. "You that Steele boy, ain't you? Livin' with Levi, right? Ain't that just the shit."

"No," Steele lied ineffectively, "that's not me."

"Well, you just tell Levi that Darryl Cooper says hi. I knew Jake back in high school. Ain't seen Jake in forever, sumpm' like five or six years anyhow. All you Steele boys look the same."

"That's not me," Steele denied his family ties again, didn't want word getting back to Papa would know Steele lied, one of Papa's worst offenses. Last time Papa discovered Steele's dishonesty he lost TV for a month, the most severe punishment Steele suffered. Chris finished stuffing his gear and jumped hurriedly to help Steele.

"No matter who you are. Get your crap outta here," Darryl threatened with a menthol coolness and the gun slightly elevated. They scrambled to the road, watched him drive off and caught him repeating, "Ain't that just the shit," shaking his head.

"Now what?" Steele defeatedly asked.

Chris shrugged.

"It's almost 9, getting dark," Steele surveyed the sky, some stars emerging. Too late to walk home, and still a couple hours before the moonrise.

"Let's hide our bags over there past the store and come back. I'm not leaving until I hear the fiddler, or stay up all night waiting for him." Chris didn't wait for Steele's response, aiming the direction they came, past the general store and café on Center Road. They stashed the backpacks in the woods, crossed a field to the creek and followed the water flow south to the bridge again, remaining out of sight behind the darkened volunteer fire station, staying mostly quiet. Listening.

Steele's mind echoed R.E.M.'s lyrics from Murmurs, *a waste of time, sitting still.* Michael Stipe's voice stroking sincerity and obscurity in veiled lyrics. What would Papa think of those lyrics? Probably call them nonsense, tell Stipe to rhyme or at least pull a real story together.

Did he look like Papa, like Barrel Darryl said, Steele wondered? Jacob looked like me, or me like him, whichever way, in the old yearbook pictures, that was true.

A waste of time, sitting still.

Chris clenched and unclenched fists besides Steele. His throbbing veins resurfaced.

Dampness seeped around, the canopy above sheltering them from early dew.

Mosquitoes swarmed like vultures on a freshly hit opossum.

Occasional cars rattled the bridge; humming over the asphalt before and after the bridge.

Trees cracked randomly. Bats fluttered overhead, random splashes from the creek hinted at brown trout feeding.

The creek bubbled and splashed, moving yet going nowhere. Water came, water went, the creek remained.

A waste of time, sitting still, Stipe's voice echoed.

A waste of time, sitting still.

A car rattling the steel bridge rattled Steele. He'd fallen asleep.

Chris was gone.

INSIDE, OUT OF CONTROL
2000 Four

With Drew in the men's room completing the final phase of the process begun at the brewery, Steele ordered another round from the bartender, mostly as an excuse to talk with her, see her perfect teeth as she smiled and watch her rhythmically glide down the bar. Such a welcome relief from the fiasco in the afternoon—an event he'd rather forget completely.

Drew snapped Steele's attention back. "I finally got to Oriole Mills Road, but much later than I hoped. Poking around in that rotting cabin took more time than I thought. Luckily Josiah Bateman drove past and gave me a ride. Remember him, blond guy, built like a walrus? Heard he joined the Army and is in Egypt at a military base now."

Steele shrugged, he'd not bothered to keep up with Josiah's life trajectory—nor anyone else from high school, except Drew. The bartender dug ice, flexing forward, her ponytail dropping off her neck to the left.

"Anyhow, he'd been smoking pot, windows up, so I got high in his car. Couldn't avoid it. I didn't want to go home—I didn't want my parents to know I was high or that I left the camping trip. He dropped me off in town, and I sat on a bench opposite Betty's house. Staring. Man, the colors of that house jumped when my mind cartwheeled in the clouds.

"I don't know how long I sat there, time fluctuated when I was stoned. Maybe an hour, or forty-five minutes? Betty noticed me sitting there, as a teacher she knew the THC gaze—I see it all the time in my students.

"Betty waved me over to her door. She asked me what I was doing, staring at her house at that hour. I couldn't answer, just smiled and giggled a bit, but the smell of stew wafted over to me and the munchies took hold. She asked if I wanted some food. So I went in."

To the collective knowledge of the town, Drew had been the first person to enter her house, and the last—his local celebrity piqued early like a maple tree bursting red in August—his legend rooted in one single event; embellished mythic retellings obfuscated the actual events of *That Night*. T. Steele, Ph.D., Assistant Professor of History, eager to ferret out truth from creative iterations, resolved to dig deep. "What did you see from the doorway, Drew?" Steele prodded. Accounts of bleached animal skulls lining the front hallway, beaded curtains made from teeth on strings, and zigzagging patterns of dog femurs alternating in black and white rows on the ceiling circulated among the decades of rumors.

"Curtains. A mishmash of curtains over the walls. Some shiny, some striped, nothing that looked new—like the Stormville Flea Market vomited rejects on her walls." Steele admired how Drew's language blossomed with each additional beer.

"Did you see anything on the walls behind them?"

"Just a peak, when I left in the morning. A jade and black zebra pattern."

"Tell me about the food. Where did you eat?"

"Past the curtains, to the left, in the kitchen. She hung a beaded curtain in the doorway, made of shells she said came from Togo." Drew gulped his beer.

"Flavors also pop when I'm high, despite the cottonmouth. She asked if I liked carrots and I despise them, so she didn't put any in my bowl. She seemed to add a dash of something, I couldn't tell what, before handing me the food. She didn't touch it. Said she just finished eating before I came inside."

The rumors about her kitchen suggested shelves overflowed with trash, scattered cat feces, that roaches danced with decomposing animal parts. "What was her kitchen like?" Steele prompted.

"A normal kitchen. Stove, fridge, oven, you know. No microwave that I noticed. Jars of homemade canned goods circled the kitchen above the cabinets in a rainbow pattern. Red fruit jams started near the door to the back porch, pickled carrots next; then corn, then asparagus, green beans, cucumber pickles; blueberry jam and grape jam near the shell curtain to the hallway. Fascinated me at the time, it was so vivid. Jars of various sizes, some oil bottles with herbs or grasses scattered around too.

"And drying plants hanging upside down all over. Under the cabinets, from the light shade, from the ceiling. I wasn't too tall then, but dodged a few of these plants to get to the table. And behind the jars, a line of drying meat."

"What kind of meat?"

"I have no idea. Strung along, like those cheap Happy Birthday signs." Odd, but not unusual if she's canning and drying her own provisions, Steele justified.

"Was it clean?"

"Save for some dishes in the sink, yeah. TV show clean, in fact." Drew paused for a minute, sipped the beer.

A Victorian house floor plan sent the gossips abuzz with possibilities. Hidden chambers housing mummified rabbits. Taxidermied tigers. Bedrooms turned closets with her matching ensembles. A reptilian ecosystem in lieu of a dining room. A bewitched basement of bubbling barrels. Twirling mobiles of crude medical instruments. Aging spell books besides 18th century English grammar tomes. Acrid hints of formaldehyde and sage. Even a grisly warlock, locked in since Vietnam. "I know you left in the morning, so you spent the night."

"Yeah. Hey, Steele, I need to get going soon." The clock approached one, with the bartender's workload clearly descended from her evening's peak of five customers. Steele realized neither he nor Drew could safely drive.

"Let's stay here," Steele suggested.

"This dump? Rooms by the hour? No telling if they clean the sheets in these rooms. I'm drunk, but not wasted."

"I'll get you a taxi. Don't worry."

"Actually, I moved into a place on Orchard. I'll stumble home," Drew insisted.

Steele signaled the bartender. "One more round, please, and some waters too." With a forced smile, she bounced down to the taps and offered up freshened mugs.

"She put something in that food, Steele. I don't know what it was, but all I recall after eating are glimpses of the night, snatches of dreams. You ever have sleep paralysis?"

Steele shook his head, doubling his dizziness.

"Your eyes open, but you can't move. Can't talk. Feels like a weight on your chest."

Steele didn't comprehend. "Like you're floating above your body?"

The bartender glanced back at the pair. Often, it seemed to Steele. But, it took two to trade glances

"No. Still in your body. Can feel your hands, legs, everything. Simply no response to moving. Nothing you can do. Like being dead, but alive."

Steele shook his head again. The last of the bar's other patrons left.

"I don't know how else to describe it. Anyhow, that's how the night went. Last I remember from being fully awake was the stew. Then glimpses, a couple seconds each time.

"First, a wall of books, old books, leather bindings, musty smell. Kinda like that shelf Papa wouldn't let you touch." The pinging of absence pierced Steele's chest, but he focused on Drew for the moment instead of Papa's passing. "I sat on a chair opposite the books in a wide, purple velvet low armchair."

"Another time, heard Green Onions by Booker T. and the MG's—I didn't know what the song was called then, but when I heard it years later in a movie it triggered the memory. More of that green and black zebra pattern on the walls, a large glass globe on a table, and Betty peering into it in a trance.

"Then I'm on the floor. Facing the wall. No noise. Looking at a case of dried animal parts, vases and cans with fur and bones poking over.

"Next time I glimpse a room, there's a towering lava lamp— maybe four feet tall. Green wax, black base, the lava floating and sinking. She's on top of me. Can't tell if I'm in her or not. Can't even remember if my pants were on. She's grinding, undulating, wearing nothing. Yelling TIGRESS, TAKE THY SEED. That green and black zebra pattern tattooed on her chest, thighs, stomach, everywhere you can't see when she's in school. Nothing I can do. She's bouncing, arching and rolling her eyes back—green eyes—then bent over me, all turned black when her limp breasts covered my face." The bartender unabashedly hovered nearby eavesdropping.

"I woke up on a couch, sun was up. Could feel my limbs, control them finally. And I ran, peaked behind those curtains on my way out."

"Describe the room you woke up in. Do you remember it?"

"Not much. I just wanted to get out of there. Those mismatched garage sale curtains covered most of the wall, although a stuffed tiger's head stared at me from between a set of Wizard of Oz curtains. Eyes threatening like it could leap off the wall at any moment."

"How did you move around in the house?"

"I don't remember. Really, I have no idea."

"That's a lot of detail for being high, then drugged too," Steele skeptically questioned.

"Yeah. I've played this over and over in my head hundreds of times. Can't say all the details are one hundred percent accurate." Drew grinned slyly. "But they're close." He sipped the water, left half a beer, hurried off to dispense more of the night's drinks.

Steele settled the tab, passing along a generous tip, and she arranged a room for him upstairs, attic level. Best for hangovers, she suggested, since it had no windows.

"When do you go back to the city?"

"Not sure, until the estate settles a bit, at least a week. Maybe two."

"Thanks for the beer. I'm buying next time. See you." They hugged an embrace of friendship, lingering half a second longer than usual, Drew's expression of condolence for Steele's loss.

The bartender rounded the counter, touched his thigh, and led Steele upstairs.

GREASE OF PASSAGE
1974, September

It's like a whole damn other language when Ranger talks, Jake thought. Jointee, juice man, Jenny, floater, talker, ride jock. Words, probably picked up from his folks since Ranger'd grown up in carnival work. Home was the road. Spent his winters near Tampa, in Gibsonton, plannin' the next season with his core group, by mid-January already itchin' to move.

At Jake's first jump after the Dutchess County Fair, Ranger set him lookin' for light bulb grease. He'd never heard of it and assumed light bulb grease would be easy to find, and circled round asking the ride jocks. Jake since learned that ride jocks understood Ranger's code when he sent green help on the pointless chase. Guys Ranger guessed would stay went to find light bulb grease; the guys Ranger thought wouldn't last a week chased Big Joe; and the ones he wasn't sure of he sent on a quest for dragon's breath. Ranger'd only been wrong twice in almost thirty years. The ride jocks circled greenies in a set pattern.

"I ain't got none, check with the Portland Plummet."

"Nope, you check the Round Raleigh?"

"No, used it all up already. The Cali Coaster's always got some."

"No. The Sacramento Swings use a ton. Go there—and what the hell's goin' on with your voice? You ain't hit puberty yet?"

Jake ignored him, wanting to bring the light bulb grease and not plant his fist in a face on his first week.

Falling short on the light bulb grease at the last ride, the final jock pointed him to the Portland Plummet.

"I already went there. Where the fuck do you get light bulb grease?" Jake slouched, defeated.

"Just go tell Ranger we don't got none. Ran out in Wilkes-Barre."

Ranger stumped out a cigarette, lit another between his stained middle and ring fingers. "You ain't gonna find it." Jake never seen no one else who smoked with those two fingers.
"I'll find it, gimme a car, I'll go to town."

"No, you ain't gonna find it. Ain't no such thing as light bulb grease. Just wanted to see how long till you come back is all. Some greenies take three hours, come back with motor oil, or just disappear. You come back in an hour, told me the truth. Now, the gates gonna open, go work Big Eli today." Jake's sensed his grit impressed the old carny.
Jake hesitated. "The what?"

"The Round Raleigh. The Ferris wheel, with Scotty. Scotty'll get you goin'." Ranger smiled, his teeth the yellow of rotting lemons as he cigarette holding fingers.

MIDWAY
1981

Pac-Man passion tsunamied the games, kids clamored for oversized knock-off plush ghosts and cheery yellow circular prizes from bottle ring toss to milk cans and balloon darts. Jake hadn't witnessed this frenzy in nearly a decade on the circuit, Ranger told him it was shapin' up to be a record sales year—and they'd each get a nice chunk of cash just before the winter break. When Jake first strayed into Ranger's world, Ranger sensed the kid's wanderlust fit in like cotton candy. Jake hadn't disappointed, he swallowed Ranger's hook like a ten-year-old spittin' daddy's money at the basketball toss.

Jake spent the first couple years figuring out the basic rules of minting money the carny way. Keeping the rides working overtaxed his mechanical instincts, sending local inspectors' away with pockets more overinflated than the basketballs.

Ranger'd treated him good, sharing his own trailer with Jake early on. Ranger explained unwritten beliefs in the carny camp when Jake started out. "Get drunk any night, but be ready to work in the mornin'. Miss work, get out. I don't take no crap. Last night of the stand, that's when you get real wasted. Guys' that been with us longest set up camp closest to the toilet. You stayin' with me, that's an exception. Once ya on your own, you'll be a quarter mile away from the john. Use a pee can, don't go pissin' next to no one's tent."

Ranger set Jake straight on women. "Don't touch no one's girlfriend—once you seen them spinnin' on Big Eli, hands off 'er. You get yourself a carny marriage too, if you want.

"And don't go messin' with no townies neither. Flirtin's fine, but don't touch. They're sure great to look at all day long, asses hangin' out them short shorts and tits poppin' outta them tank tops. I've seen hundred's of 'em bust loose in the bumper cars, you'll be seein' that too." Ranger'd noticed the local ladies talkin' to Jake like flies on candy apples, his blonde curls and green eyes a combo he ain't never seen on no guy before.

Ranger kept tearing along. "Girls'd come round the camp, same girls each place, they know when we're in town. Most ain't nuthin' to look at, but use your mind from whoever you'd seen that day. Treat 'em right, pay 'em good. Just like the talkers buildin' up a tip to the crowd, each has her specialty way of doin' things. You get it. We jump, they hump."

"Ain't no law against takin' in a yokel, right?" Jake's mind flashed to a brunette that gave him her number on a hot dog tray that afternoon.

"Ain't no law, sure; but you knock one up and you get your ass sued for child support. They'll find you, or their lawyers will. Just leave'm alone, you'll be alright." Ranger lost many good hands because they couldn't pay for their unwanted brats, 'specially after he started gettin' legit with taxes and all.

Passing stuffed yellow plushes, Jake remembered chasing light bulb grease himself, having just sent a greenie looking for Big Joe two hours ago and not seeing him yet. Predictable. The guys think they wanna travel but won't leave their beds, girlfriends, parents, or pets. They ain't got conviction, once they seen fourteen hour workdays, standin' in sun, sleepin' in tents, they figure they'll go back to school or work construction and stick around their towns. They sort themselves out, for the most part.

Back in Dutchess County again, in Rhinebeck. Wanting to keep away from the crowds, knowing Levi always came for the apple judging, he figured the boy would be tall enough for the rides this year. With setup complete, he left the fair until tear down, as agreed with Ranger since his first year back.

Ranger'd shown Jake 'bout the rides, dealin' with the advance team, keepin' sideshow acts fresh, workin' patches with local cops, keepin' the concession managers in line and honest, watchin' for signs of oachin' from the game jointees—'specially now that Ranger'd bought 'em out and ran them too. Like Big Eli comin' together, Jake rose above the crew to Ranger's second in command.

First year the company circled back to Dutchess County, Ranger told Jake to take off. Everyone's gonna need time away during the gruelin' months, Ranger told him, and they all get distracted when near their homes thinkin' of parents or kids or friends or old haunts, so best to let 'em loose.

Jake avoided the Hudson riverside—memories of Ka flowed in its waters, thoughts Jake drowned to the bottom and killed with the PCBs, a tumor of his past.

The cabin lured Jake, a silent game talker ensnared him into its hidden recesses. He and Levi built it from logs they felled, moss they collected together and stuffed between logs; the only project he clearly remembered his father working on with his hands; built on land Jake considered theirs, belonging to the family for over a century—rightfully they should still own it. Not that it mattered none now. Deep in the forest when the show looped back, he welcomed the quiet escape.

When he and Levi built the cabin they first dug the pit. Levi showed Jake how to shovel the square without walls collapsing, throwing soil to a mound several feet away, now rounded from time and rain and litterfall. They lined the bottom and sides with slate relocated from a nearby Dutch boundary wall, Levi rambling about the Dutch legacy surrounding them, cementing over the rocks. They hauled in an iron cellar door, *illillilli* etched across, drilled into the cement with hand tools to frame and bolt it in place. They placed a drum stove on the cellar door.

Drugs no longer interested him—carnival thrills altered his mind now. The bright gaudiness of lights flashing their fantastic patterns fueled his blood, weed glued him to a seat. His heart beat with the rhythm of hissing pistons and high arcs of steel frames and cages. Frightened screams of teenage girls—and their 'courageous' boys—spiked his adrenaline; no substance he ever inhaled, injected, swallowed, absorbed, or snorted propelled him as quickly, or left so cleanly.

Once at the cabin, another cacophony of sounds overtook Jake's senses. The chorus of early morning songbirds. Rushes of air bending branches, brushing leaves together and away. Sticks snapping beyond sight. Fire crackling in the evening. Rain pounding—or gently tapping—the aluminum roof. Blaze of the morning sun, dusks' violent purples, pinks and oranges clashing and erased by patternless distant stars.

His calloused hands toyed the key retrieved from its hidden spot beneath the stove, fixed in a magnetic box all these seasons. The last time they left the cabin together Levi told Jake to go out and wait while he finished up inside. When Levi delayed, Jake peeked seeing his father on hands and knees reaching beneath the stove. Around ten years old then, a couple years older than the boy now.

The boy. Jake struggled to drown thoughts of the boy with Ka in the river, but the boy wouldn't disappear with her. He resurfaced at this cabin. Had Levi brought the boy here? The cabin looked neglected since his last visit, brush growing beside the walls and moss spreading over the door.

The boy's presence somewhere nearby—perhaps experiencing his first coaster this minute, maybe simply throwing a ball around with friends in a yard—penetrated Jake's thoughts. Jake's burden of abandoning the boy tore fierce fire in his soul. Seeking distractions Jake set rabbit traps, hiked the ridge, collected wild raspberries; but this year the boy seeped into Jake as never before.

Maybe Jake should drop this soul-searching crap, just stick with the company. They'd do fine without him one week, for sure, but did he really need this quiet break? The lies he told—or didn't tell—Ranger about why he took the week off started to grow. Ranger prodded just a bit about what he did during this week when they left Wilkes-Barre, questions Jake deflected with a quick, "Nothin' really. Concessions got slammed, eh?" That drove Ranger to review the jump's good and could-be-betters.

Fishing trout with a cane pole and worms, Jake immersed himself in sounds of the creek, trying to shake off the boy's shadow in his head.

"Well, ain't that the shit. Jacob Steele, jus' sittin' there fishin'. Ain't seen this SOB in what, eight, nine years, and you's just tryin' to catch trout like Sunday mornin' with Norman Rockwell. Where the hell you been, man?" The bellow jolted Jake from his trance. The guy probably doubled in size since they last sat in Betty's classroom together. Jake grasped for his name.

He forced out his practiced grin, the one to put a mommy at ease when her 42-½ inch child climbs into her first Daytona Dash ride. "Darryl Cooper, how the hell are ya'? It's been a long fuckin' time. What the hell you doin' these days?" Jake eased with his animated beaver voice.

"Little of this, little of that. Some folks payin' me to watch over their land, keep trespassers out. Now, you gonna need to git goin', y'know. No fishin' or huntin' allowed no more. This is private land. Been that way for a while. What the hell you up to?"

Jake gave part truth, "drivin' trucks cross country," fuming under his calm answer

"Where to?"

"All over, mostly East Coast, Florida to Maine, round the South."

"Well, ain't that just the shit. I ain't been no further than Hartford, and down to Atlantic City once. Lost my balls in blackjack—well, lost a thousand bucks in blackjack, my wife nearly took off my balls. Married Alice Elba, 'member her?"

How long is he gonna hang around, Jake wondered. "Alice with short black hair and mushroom shaped ears, that one?" And smelled like day old, fly covered largemouth bass in the sun.

Darryl poked more. "Got us twin girls and a boy. You got kids?"

He shrugged. "Life on the road, not sure." Jake pulled his empty line from the water. "Hey, Darryl, who owns this land now?"

"I ain't allowed to say. Jus' that they like them privacy, is all. But I can't stop ya from goin' to town hall, neither. How's your father doin'?"

"Alright." Jake didn't know more or less about his father anyhow; he plastered on the carny smirk again. "You all take good care of them kids. Bring 'em to the fair, I hear it's the best in years.

"I'll get off this land, no worries, Darryl. Ain't gotta tell me twice." Fuckin' idiot. It should be his land, if his father hadn't screwed him over.

Darryl Cooper teetered off to the west, Jake to the north just to throw him off his real trail.

It dawned on Jake when he couldn't hear Darryl's thudding no more— Darryl Cooper married Alice Elba. That guy's wife is Alice Cooper.

As Jake returned to the cabin, he realized only severed connections remained in Red Hook. He knew nothin' of his father or the boy. People from school days marrying up and havin' mushroom-eared babies. School's out, for sure.

Jake fumed. Kicked off his family's land. Screw town hall, it didn't matter no more. He stuffed his clothes into the duffel bag, launched lawn chairs across the room. Shot-putted a table through the only window, dropping his blade. That damned stove came out of his grandfather's house. Let it fucking rust here, dammit. Disappear like this goddamn family. His pounding kicks dislodged the stovepipe, toppled the stove, spewed embers on the curtains, close to where he'd carved his name in the log.

***

"You're early, expected you in three more days." Ranger stared at Jake like a surprise safety inspector.

Jake skipped any talk of what happened. "Any problems with the Memphis Spinner? Them seat belts holdin' up?" His voice deepened a notch.

BOY AND A BRIDGE
1987, June

He'd been beside Steele, leaning on the log when Steele fell asleep. Steele felt the ground where Chris sat, the soil cold. With the moon up he could see clearly, the pale blueish light creating shadowy layers twitching in the slight breeze. Maybe he needed to piss, Steele thought, and strained for sounds of movement.

Leaves rustling. An owl hoo-hooing. The faintest puff of a car door closing outside the café down the road. Distant dogs duetting. The creek tinkling its secret messages. No footsteps or twigs snapping.

He stood, peered across the bridge, spotted a fluttering, suspended mass about fifteen feet beyond the overpass. Shadows and branches obscured its shape. Urged to move closer, the voice that warned him earlier not to join his friends reached his ears again. *NO*, it shushed, no.

Blood throbbed in his ears, each heartbeat ticking quicker, stronger, louder. Bangs pasted to his clammy forehead, the stench of fear's sweat already reeking as he ducked under the low bridge, through the shallow water and over slick worn rocks. Past the bridge an icy cloud enveloped his right side as he cautiously edged towards the floating form.

He stopped, heard a faint high pitch draw from somewhere nearby. A slow, disappointed whine, barely audible beneath the creek's splashes. Or maybe he imagined the droning, driven by the legend and his hypersensitive condition? He paused to listen more closely, and to study the suspended oblong shape.

Somber stringed notes resonated more clearly, close to the fleeting form, along the stream bank. The notch in his abdomen swelled.

The shape meandered amid the branches towards the source of the music, towards the road. Branches and leaves entered it undisturbed like fog, the form surrounding the vegetation, then it pivoted back towards the creek. Towards Steele. It swayed between two points several times, seemingly trapped in its place. As it silently vacillated above, the water flowed around his feet, and he felt drawn towards it, as if it beckoned Steele to follow. Maybe Chris found this and followed it too.

CRACK!

The gunshot vanquished all noises, left a deafening, steady tone in his ears, and he dove into shrubs. A forceful grip circled his bicep—not too difficult with his stringy arms—and weeded Steele out from the bushes, dragging him halfway to the road where Steele dropped.

"Well, ain't that just the shit," Darryl paused, panting. "Your buddy's up in my truck. I'm gonna take you boys through the police station, and let your folks come and pick you up. They ain't gonna like that shit, no way. I told you to git home, and ya didn't, so now you're in deep. Stay here." He tottered downhill again, reached beneath some leaves and pulled out a small hidden small cassette player. "Bet you thought ya heard the fiddler, huh? I told you, ain't no fiddler, that's all bull. This thing'll go for eight hours on fresh batteries, play one side then flip to the other, back n forth. I put it there when I think the fiddler's gonna git some visitors."

Steele searched the branches for the form but it had vanished. If he really saw anything. He began to doubt. He pointed up to the area anyhow, "What was up there?"

Darryl looked confused, as if he couldn't tell if Steele was just plain stupid or trying to distract him. He glanced up. "It's the damn moon, boy," then mumbled and shook his head, "ain't that just the shit, camping alone out here and don't even know what the damn moon is." The gun's barrel shifted towards the pickup. "Git on up there. Damn too much like Jake, tresspassin' and all like I caught him a few years back. Ain't that just the shit." He huffed, hoisting himself into the driver's seat.

HALF TUBE OF MINTS
2000 Five

Momentary panic swept over Steele when he opened his eyes, wondering what town he woke up in, why and how he'd gotten there; the alien yellowed walls, threadbare area rug, blinking alarm clock, the VHF/UHF TV dials, and a bed of chunks and divots. His head pounded fiercely, stomach ready to turn out its contents.

He recollected Drew's story at the bar of *That Night*—Betty drugging and mounting him for the Tigress. And the knife and key Drew found *That Night* in the burnt cabin. They'd combed through that ruin a dozen other times before and after *That Night* and never found anything. Nor did Drew ever mention those pieces. These two objects possibly held stories for Steele, perhaps about his family, but where to begin?

A couple long, thick ebony hair strands ribboned on the pillow beside him, with Rosa's name and phone number in tidy handwriting on scrappy hotel letterhead.

After a delicate drive, then a beer to taper the hangover's sting, Steele entered his childhood room with its R.E.M. posters, a virtual discography of their 1980s releases plastering the walls, Out of Time the most recent, including fan club Christmas gifts on the shelves.

As a teen he clung to their every song, every album, listening for clues about the larger world beyond Red Hook and Rhinebeck. Receiving that package each December masked the void of parental gifts. He slid *Green* out of its shell and into the dual cassette deck, hoping at least one unit still functioned. Jangling guitars and the lyrics of lost memories echoed. His throbbing head could use silence, but his spirit needed grounding in the familiar.

The cassette auto-flipped several times as Steele waded through more of Papa's treasures. Mike Mills and Michael Stipe's yearning interplayed on the untitled final song, triggering flashes of Rosa in the night, him holding her and her holding him.

Steele turned over the knife and key, now able to see them in detail in the daylight. Deeply etched on the blade Lady Liberty stood tall, welcoming the masses. A small boat of immigrants approached her. Waves surrounded her and the boat. A scene of optimism, of hope. Scuffmarks verified this as a utility knife for its previous owner, as did the remaining jiggered bone handle, smoothed from routine grip and polished from its owner's hand oils. The jagged initials JS etched on the reverse side certainly were added after manufacturing.

The key surrendered no information. Perhaps a crusty old locksmith with decades of experience might glean something from its shape, some clue for what kind of lock it pairs with. He looped it to a silver neck chain Papa wore infrequently, draping it around his neck.

The dense and pungent odor redolent of labored breathing and soiled sheets greeted Steele in Papa's room. He rarely stepped in there when growing for fear of discovering unwanted secrets—it felt as distant as the 1940s. Stillness of the recently departed lingered there, clinging to the space. Clothes expecting to be worn, a watch waiting for a wrist, slippers ready to warm his feet, half a foil tube of mints on top of the dresser; Steele could never remember him with a new tube, or just one mint— always midway through the pack as if it regenerated itself in his pocket. Overwhelmed at the thought of sorting out this room, he slowly paced, indecisively nudged items atop the furniture.

Papa's closet beckoned. Just a simple closet, two sliding doors protected an eight-foot long cavity two feet deep. Shirts and pants crammed in on hangers, some winter jackets stuffed along the left wall; a stack of shoeboxes along the right wall arranged from widest on the bottom to smallest on top. He could start there, he supposed.

The box stacks triggered old insecurities and anxieties that Steele suppressed long ago. As Steele grew taller Jacob's wake widened. The chasm from being abandoned as an infant distanced him from himself in adolescence, his intensity and early embers of self-awareness focused on the missing rather than the present.

As he reached for the top box when his cell phone vibrated.

"Hello?" An unfamiliar number displayed on the caller ID.

"Steele, this is Rosa. Are you free now?"

Steele paused a moment to place the name. Rosa, the note from the hotel. His cheeks reddened. He never picked up a woman in a bar for a one-night tangle before. Either the alcohol or a fleeting urge to fill a void consumed him, he reasoned with himself. He didn't recall giving out his number, though. "Um, sure. I'm just…well," he glanced at the box tower, "yeah."

"Where are you? I'll come there."

Rosa arrived, looking luscious; a red tulip emerging from a late winter snow. Steele found no other words to describe her. They hugged, an awkward hug of paradoxically intimate strangers. She started, peering straight into his eyes, "Look, last night. I never do that. I mean, I've never just taken a guy for a one-night stand. I'm not normally that kind."

Steele nodded, mesmerized by her mahogany brown eyes, so dark they appeared black.

"But, there was something about you. You stared at me from the second you stepped through the door. What did you see?," she challenged him.

"Um, honestly," would Steele be honest with her? "You. A vivid, striking, gorgeous woman. Confident, anticipating all your customers' moves before they did. That showed me intelligence too. That bar is your realm. Before Drew—that's my friend—

before he arrived, I wondered what brought you to the hamlet of Rhinecliff, wanted to know about you and your story; then he came and we drank too much. Way too much. The beer trumped the brain, and carnal urges buried my questions." Honestly laid out.

She surveyed the living room flowing into the dining room-turned-library, its jumbled boxes and shelves of books; its velveteen Kelly green semi circle sectional sofa, dusty from the chain of years when Papa could no longer maintain the house; 1980s loose shag carpet with mowed tracks to the kitchen, down the hall, and from the entrance. "Right, well, since we're being true with each other, I wasn't drunk—I never drink on the job— but my keg hadn't been tapped in a while, and there you were, obviously eager. Right time, right place for you." She smirked, and half winked. "So, is this your place?" She spoke with a staccato beat.

"No, well, yes. Well, I'm not certain, yet." Steele explained an attorney would meet him in a couple days to review Papa's will.

"So, you're not sure of your inheritance, what about your parents? Aunts and uncles? Siblings?" Innocent questions, with complex answers. His forehead wrinkled. The lingering sting of abandonment needled him again. Steele blandly walked through the basics of being raised by Papa, as if his 813th time doing so, to veer around the emotions.

"You're likely to inherit whatever he owned?" Disbelief tinged her curt tone.

Steele nodded imperceptibly. Likely not much beyond this drooping house to inherit, neglected as the Dutch stone dwellings of his and Papa's fascinations.

"Need help?" she gestured around the house.

"Why are you here, though?" Steele probed.

"Well, you're cute for one," she reached a hand to his stomach tilted her head back to bridge the gap in their heights, "and secondly, to give you another chance. I'm hoping you can improve on that lackluster performance."

CLEANSING
2000 Six

They purged the pantry, unearthing canned goods Warhol might have immortalized in his prime, scrubbed dishes crusted with indistinguishable brown sauces, set the oven to self clean, and cut through a quarter inch of stove top detritus. The freezer unveiled frozen foods that expired a decade earlier. The dishwasher churned for five cycles just to ensure all plates, cups, and silverware wouldn't sicken anyone in the new millennium.

Conversation clicked between her work and his research—her questions hinted at genuine interest in the history of the region. They trampled over topics from the Yankees to yard work; sandwiches to pets (both quixotically hunting the 'perfect pastrami' while mystified by 'pet people', especially doggy devotion). Five hours later the kitchen gleamed, and Steele's intrigue now drilled far deeper than the superficial attraction at the bar. Eventually the topic strayed back to his upbringing.

"You never met them, then?"

"No," he hesitated.

"Have you ever tried to find them?"

"When I was a teen I desperately wanted to know them. I'd fantasize about life with them—how it might have been to grow up with a mother and father like most of my friends here. To be normal." He briefly thought of Chris, and his unsolved disappearance *That Night*, thirteen years ago; how Chris's idyllic family collapsed like their shoddy, makeshift fort in the woods after a strong thunderstorm the day after *That Night*. "But I've grown past that, come to accept that my journey is mine alone; Marika and Jacob chose to live their lives regardless of the collateral damage. The Universe presents its eternal mysteries as opportunities masked behind challenges." He noticed Rosa slightly stiffen while he philosophized; something in that statement seemed to strike her. "Thanks for the help today, Rosa. Mr. D's pastrami is B-rated, for an Italian place in the sticks, believe it or not. Let's go get some."

She glanced at her watch, nodded non-committedly but distractedly. "Steele, you're hollow. There's a gaping void in your being, and it's moldering at the edges. It's peculiar, but for extraordinary souls I see auras; not with my eyes but with my spirit. When you walked into the bar last night I merged with your soul for an instant." He believed her, a sensation of present awareness flashed over him when he entered the bar, which he read for nostalgia at the time, but an unsettled anxiety also accompanied the warm comfort. She continued, "and again this morning in this house, I felt it stronger. You need to find them, Steele, find the tincture to reverse the decay. And…" she dug deep into herself, the anxious energy vibrations reverberating, "and another loss as well. One you feel responsible for, a deep sense of regret burdens you." She peered deeper, merged into his being. "We'll do this together."

He crumbled into a wallow of tears for the second time in his life, and with a near stranger. She dove into his darkest crevices, areas he failed to scrub with years of therapy. All those powerful healing workshops at the Alpha Institute of Spirituality only superficially concealed the wounds Rosa excised in a few minutes. She knew. She just knew.

And now Steele admitted to himself, finally. Since *That Night* he intuited that he must pursue Marika and Jacob both.

She stood suddenly and tenderly squeezed his hand, then drove them to Mr. D's. She rated the pastrami at B- due to soggy sauerkraut; he scored it a solid B with the fresh rye and homemade mustard. The great A+ pastrami sandwich remained at large.

DISCARDED
1987, June

His sneakers soaked, skin itched from poison ivy and mosquitos. Anxiety amplified his physical discomfort. Drew's tantrum, Chris's anger at his father's affair, Chris gone missing, and this Darryl guy saying he talked with Jacob within the past few years. Steele opened the door to the 1985 Chevy pickup and climbed in the passenger seat. Darryl opened his door, the whole truck tilting to the left when he heaved himself behind the wheel. "Damn, where'd that boy go?" Chris must have split when Darryl chased Steele out from the stream. "I shoulda tied him up. You got any ideas?"

"No. But we left our stuff around the corner. Can I get mine before you take me home?" The engine ripped across the soundscape, dousing the night's beauty with a petroleum-fueled roar.

"Don't try nothin' funny, boy. Ol' Levi gonna be pissed already, you don't want him no more flustered."

Steele jumped out and found his bag. Chris's bag remained in the same place, but looked like it vomited its contents just like Halloween bounty dumped on the living room floor. "Um, Mr. Cooper?" He pointed to the spread out mess. "Something's not right."

Darryl toddled over. "You ain't done that, boy?" Steele

denied with a headshake. His arms itched intensely from the developing rash and bites, and all he wanted now was to get home for a shower and a coating of calamine lotion, despite the whooping Papa would rain on him. "Then he been here. Took whatever he wanted and ran off. Ain't that just the shit." Darryl examined the leaves, saw Chris's tracks angled at a V back to the road towards town. "If he run on the road, ain't no way I'm gonna track him, not at night no how. You pick up his crap, let's git goin'. I'm gonna keep my eyes on you." He picked up Steele's backpack effortlessly, like a bag of donuts.

Chris took only the food. As far as Steele could tell all the clothes and camping gear remained. Could have been an opossum, a raccoon, or some other animal, but Steele guessed Darryl would see those tracks.

Leaning over to open the front passenger door for Steele, Darryl's portly hand explored the seat's crevice while his eyes searched down the road with high beams on. He thundered, "NOW, AIN'T THAT JUST THE SHIT!" and tore through the glove box, between the seats, under the mats. "YOU AIN'T SEEN IT, DID YOU?" Steele, alarmed by Darryl's rising anger, had no clue what he searched for and shrugged calmly. "MY PISTOL'S GONE. YOUR FRIEND STOLE IT!" Steele stood unmoving, blank look on his face, skin burning. If he didn't get washed off soon, the allergic reaction would set in. Last summer poison ivy spread into his throat and he couldn't speak for a week, staying on an I.V. steroid drip in Upper County Hospital for five days.

A police cruiser arrived and cut its lights. A slim lady approached them from the café's direction, drawn out by the red and blue lights. Her youthful years clearly behind her, she retained an elegance in her sharp features, hair pulled into a graying ponytail. The bored looking cop started towards Darryl and the lady targeted Steele.

"What are you doing out here, young man?" She questioned Steele.

"Well, my friend and I, we wanted to—" Steele strained to explain.

She cut in with a hushed tone, "Wanted to hear the fiddler? Did you?"

Steele didn't respond. How did she know?

"Did you see him? Hear him?" Her strong, calm voice pierced him like a velvet nail.

"No...well," Steele angled his chin towards Darryl, "he put a tape recorder under some leaves with fiddle music playing, so no, I didn't hear the fiddler."

She leaned over to whisper to him. "He's there. Hard to hear, but I've heard him. Not everyone will hear his music, or see him in the branches. He only reveals himself to those that are open. He wants to connect, to tell his story, to warn those of us who are ready to hear him not to live with regret. Did you see anything? That's my question."

Looking at the ground Steele whispered back, "In the branches, there was something moving, a ball of mist. Size of a beach ball, but kind of egg-shaped too."

Her eyes scanned him, up and down, and continued with the susurrate tone. "Next time you come out, you find me. I own the store and café, and live just beside it. I'm Julia, just go inside and ask for me."

As Darryl and the police officer finished their conversation Darryl waddled towards Steele and Julia. Julia's voice amplified to full strength. "So, the missing bike is a women's mountain bike,15 speed, red as a cardinal." Steele wondered why she ended the conversation with a different topic, not seeing the officer coming from behind him.

"Do you want to file a statement about the stolen bike?" The policeman asked mechanically.

"No, sir, could be my daughter put it somewhere it's not supposed to be. It'd be too much trouble to file a report now then find it behind the barn in the morning."

The cop spoke to Steele. "You get home, don't get in any more trouble tonight, okay?"

"Um-hmm," he quasi-agreed, sensing trouble mounting.

As events of the night thickened, Steele thought of Papa's simple lesson about the transformational nature of emergencies.

"A fire transforms wood to smoke, smoke joins clouds, clouds drop rain, and the rain waters trees that grow in the ashes. The wood suffers initially, and new life springs from it eventually. You'll have times when you despair, Thurgood, but you'll grow stronger from them." Steele hoped Papa would show some pity with the belt, keep the suffering soft this night. Even though it hung threateningly in the broom closet, Papa never used it on him. Net yet, he admitted. Steele had never before given Papa a reason to do so.

"Why are you driving so slowly? The itching's getting worse every minute," Steele complained.

"Shut up and watch for your friend," Darryl commanded, crouched forward scanning the sides of the road. Steele concentrated on not scratching. He thought he glimpsed a bike's reflector, but it turned out to be a driveway marker. Not that he would tell Darryl if he glimpsed Chris. As Darryl crawled the pickup near the marker Steele noticed a discarded Cheezey Oodles bag.

"Mr. Cooper, did you say you saw Jacob a couple years ago?"

"Yup, three or four years ago. Why?"

"Just wondering. Where was he?" Steele glanced over to Darryl, Darryl's eyes scanned left to right in the night as if reading a book. The moon dyed the landscape blue.

"Near a stream, fishin'; and on private land, trespassin', like you."

"Oh. You sure it was him?"

"Yup. All you Steele guys look the same. Wiry build, curly blonde hair, green eyes. I'd pick any of you out of a line up for sure. And his voice like he never went through puberty. I think you look more like your granddaddy than your daddy, your nose's more crooked like Mr. Steele's. I ain't seen Jake but once since he left high school, that time in the woods. He never finished school, you know, and at least I graduated. He just dropped out and run off. Ain't that just the shit, with a new baby and all." He shook his head righteously, and glanced sideways, Steele sensed pity in the look.

Papa never mentioned Jacob visiting. Steele needed to find a way to ask him.

Steele didn't want this to be true, that Jacob actually came back but didn't visit him. An anger swelled in his abdomen, a sickening feeling of nausea after a jab to his gut, his cheeks and forehead flushing garnet. He noticed his fists clenched Chris-style, then forced them to unfurl, but his right hand clutched the armrest on the door and his left squeezed the seat cushion. Steele figured he must have been about ten years old when the two grown ups crossed each other in the woods—*what could a kid have done to be discarded by his supposed father?* Steele blamed himself.

"You okay?" Darryl noticed his color change as an oncoming padiddle lit up the cab. Steele ignored him.

His skin burned with rash and bites, and his whole upper body felt like an overinflated balloon as the rage of betrayal intensified. He'd felt brief flares of hate for Jacob, yet the ferocity and veracity of discovering total and complete rejection—twice in one lifetime—one short lifetime—twice by the same man—compelled Steele to grope for the door handle.

Steele peeked at the speedometer. Darryl increased up to thirty miles per hour now, and if he timed it right the rear tire could crush him. He hoped to never feel anything. Ever. Again. Then Jacob would never know—and always wonder—what became of him. To eliminate himself from this earth would be Steele's revenge, to disappear with the finality that evaded Jacob. He tightly gripped the smooth metal lever.

Then Papa's face flashed through his mind.

Papa would be crushed. By way of blood relatives, I am all he has in the world, Steele conceded. Jacob doesn't exist to Papa; Papa repeats that to him persistently. "When Jacob left you, he created a wound in my heart that's slowly repaired itself in these years, closing him out. For many years I hoped he would return, as much for you as for me. It's you and me in this world, Thurgood, let's make life worth living well."

Papa fussed, but rarely refused anything that Steele asked for. Even when Steele showed a glancing interest in a hobby he would bring some piece of it home—which explains the untouched guitar, arrows, drum set, skateboard, snow skis, scooter, two bicycles, and the rest of the tangled clutter clogging half the garage.

Steele loosened his grip on the door handle. His fury boiled, and he began to sense how Chris felt betrayed at the golf course. Perhaps Steele might need *seven thousand years to sleep away the pain* as Michael Stipe sang in 7 Chinese Bros.

"Mr. Cooper, can you go faster? I landed in poison ivy when you shot the gun, and I'm allergic. I need to get these clothes off and shower. The itching is really, really intense."

"Well, ain't that the shit," stretching out the last syllable like savoring the first scoop of ice cream, "first your friend almost T-bones me, then you ignore my command to git off the property, then your friend steals my pistol and runs off, and now you want a favor from me to git you home? Damn, boy, you full of fun today." Sarcastic SOB, Steele thought.

The truck shimmied after a loud pop, Darryl calmly guided it to a stop near the roadside ditch overgrown with weeds.

"AIN'T THAT JUST THE SHIT! Goddam tire blew. Dammit!" His curses echoed in the cavernous cab. "Boy, you got another 30 minutes 'fore we git goin' again."

DUTCH MEXICAN
2000 Seven

"Let's take a break from this, Rosa. Do you hike?"

"It's just walking, but in the woods, right? I'll keep up."

Parking on the roadside of Hollow Road with a small daypack, they trailblazed a slow path through the spongy underbrush, the sun's warmth renewing life with optimistic growth, adolescent leaves darkening to jade, rejuvenating decaying scree into fragrant nutty, mossy aromas.

Steele paused about half an hour into the jaunt, resting on a stone wall, Rosa beside him, sharing iced tea. Soaking in signs of the life cycle all around reminded him of another of Papa's quips. "Papa insisted the ideal nutrients for apple trees consisted of compost from apple leaves and the pulp remaining from pressed cider."

"So, at our core we rejuvenate ourselves?" Rosa dove immediately into a deep metaphysical interpretation. "Each day we suffer small losses, transforming those into silage to nurture growth in our spirit. Transitions define our lives, Steele. Your Papa recognized that, he prepared you through his apple metaphors and focus on history."

Her intense spirit and perceptive observations attracted him deeper still, a trench of sapient insights harmonized Rosa's outer beauty. "Rosa, tell me how you found yourself tending bar in that dumpy hotel."

"Not much of a story to tell, really."

"Tell me. I'm all yours." Too much, too soon? His cheeks, already flush from exertion in the thick brush, darkened slightly.

"My mother died in childbirth with me, in Nogales, Mexico near the Arizona border. I'm her only daughter. My father searched for work in the maquiladoras unsuccessfully, eventually crossing the border to Tucson and finding odd jobs on construction sites between there and Phoenix. He left me with my grandmother, my mother's mother, since he couldn't take care of an infant. He sent money home, though, to support us, when he could.

"Nearby my Abuela's village a group of well intentioned people from the U.S. created a farm and a free school for local children. My father insisted that I attend that school, Escuela Esperanza, with a head teacher from the U.S.

"Around my seventh birthday, which is December fifteenth, my father visited. The head teacher and my father spoke for long that day, well after all the children went home. Eventually my father married the head teacher and we all moved to the U.S."

Steele handed her a granola bar.

"Mama looked nothing like most of the indigenous Mexicans, with her cropped hair and pale skin. Very Gringa." She puffed a short laugh. "She gave birth to two more girls, my sisters Inez and Elizabet, identical twins. Mama teaches at a rural school, now in New Mexico.

"Occasionally Mama described the land she grew up in, so vastly different from the flat, hot deserts I'd known my entire life. To me, the exotic images of tree covered hillsides, vibrant autumn leaves, claustrophobic winters, and glorious springs overwhelmed my curiosity. I always dreamed of coming here, to see it for myself." She unwrapped the bar.

"Despite my parents' insistence on education, my restlessness to wander trumped any feeble attempt to study. I tested out of high school with a GED, got my bartending certificate, and drifted west, then north to Seattle and eventually east through Boise, Helena, Fargo, Minneapolis, Madison, Pittsburgh, and ultimately here. I lied about my age until I became old enough to legally serve alcohol."

"Is this place all you imagined?" Other than a brief trip to Kansas City to present a paper at the Society for Historical Research conference, Steele's travels brought him as far east as Boston and south to Washington, D.C.

"Even better. Well, the hotel's a dump, but the owners treat me okay and customers tip well, mostly. They give me a room in addition to wages, so I don't have many bills." She waved at a fly buzzing around, even that mundane gesture entranced Steele. "All the scenery, the friendliness of people, the deep Eurocentric culture that Mama mentioned vibrate here—like a National Geographic photo in real life." She smiled paradoxically, or so Steele thought.

"Did you specifically look for Rhinebeck or Red Hook?" Steele asked

"Yes. Mama's stories made this place sound ideal, the complete opposite of my desert homes. When I first arrived here, stepping off a night bus, I sensed a comforting warmth in this alien place; dually home yet completely foreign."

"Opposites in perfect balance?" Steele prodded.

"Like decay and growth, yes. So, I've been at the hotel for about half a year. Drew comes a couple times per week, usually alone. Drinks two beers. A lousy tipper, though."

"And your wanderlust, when will you move on?" Never, he hoped to hear.

Without hesitation she offered, "when the urge strikes. I never stayed more than six months in those other places. Big cities repel me."

Deflated by her response Steele changed the topic. "Let's go explore."

The dense growth nearly obfuscated Steele's target on this trek: an abandoned Dutch foundation. "Check this out. A classic two room Dutch frame house, they built windows and doors into the walls for structural support." As Steele continued the lecture his voice grew louder, more animated, until squirrels scurried higher into the trees growing inside the forgotten dwelling. Rosa's imagination colored features of daily life of the Dutch settlers as Steele detailed them; strikingly similar to her own Mexican childhood.

BOY'S RECKONING
1987, June

"We can't go more'n thirty miles an hour on the donut, boy, now get inside and we'll roll out of here. I knew I shoulda gotten a full size spare."

Five minutes later Darryl pulled over again, Steele's clothes now irritating his skin with the slightest move.

"Ain't that just the shit. There's that lady's red bike, in front of the golf course. You think your buddy's nearby?" He exposed his yellowing teeth under a thin sneer, grabbed the shotgun from the back seat and a rectangular yellow four D battery flashlight from the floor. After the flat tire Steele remained mute. He belittled everything Steele shared all night, so Steele would just ignore him. "We're gonna go find out. C'mon, itchy britches."

Struggling to one knee, Darryl scanned the dirt near the golf course's entrance for signs, picking up a Cheezey Oodles bag. "I like his food, wish I had me some Cheezey Oodles right now. Anyhow, he gone through here, that way. Less than thirty minutes ago, I imagine." Pointing the general direction towards the path they emerged from earlier in the day, Chris's steps left obvious mars in the pristine dew-layered fairway. Darryl launched for the chase.

And stopped after four hundred feet.

"I ain't gonna catch him. I couldn't catch a turtle in molasses, let alone a damn fourteen year old runnin' like a white tailed deer. C'mon. We gonna git you home," he wheezed.

Papa popped out the door when the truck pulled into the driveway, the first time Steele saw him awake at this hour since soothing Steele during a bout of flu last winter. Levi, blinking and shielding his eyes from the truck's beams, angled towards the driver's side when Steele called him. "Papa, I've been in poison ivy and my skin is on fire. I need to get cleaned up."

Cheeks and forehead angered to the ruby color of a Cortland apple, Papa's shoulders dropped upon seeing the pair. "All right, then you have some explaining to do, Thurgood Levi Steele." As Steele entered the home he caught Papa and Darryl shaking hands with familiarity. Everyone liked Papa; everyone except Jacob, it seemed.

"Did you put your clothes in the washer?" Papa questioned him.

"Yes, everything I carried, and it's on hot with extra soap."

"Good. I hoped you knew that by now. Tell me what happened. No lies."

"Well, we started towards Miller's Pond like I told you, but we ended up going to Fiddler's Bridge."

"You planned to go to the bridge all along, didn't you?"

Quietly, Steele surveyed the bookshelves, not wanting to see Papa's face. A slight nod acknowledged the truth.

"So, you lied to me."

Droplets gathered in the corner of Steele's eyes, he avoided Papa's gaze. Embarrassment and disappointment flowed through Steele like murmurs of the stream under Fiddler's Bridge.

"Thurgood, I'm frustrated. Saddened. You know better than to lie, I know you know that. So why?"

Steele shrugged one shoulder dismissively. Talking to the carpet he muttered, "I didn't think you'd let me go. It's far."

"And you are correct, my boy. There is no way I would let you go, it's miles and miles from here." He paused. Steele wanted to tell him about the whole night in detail, especially the floating shape among the branches and what Julia whispered, but just uttering a word would push him to bawling. He locked the story away.

"You went with your friends. Are they home?" Papa grilled him.

Another shrug. "I don't know."

"Their parents called. Drew's father wanted him to wash the dog before going. We chatted and discovered you all told different stories about your plans. The cornfield, Haakinson's Orchard, Millerd's Pond, nothing matched up. They're boiling mad like a pot of applesauce, and worried. I will phone them, tell them you're fine. Where are the others?" All along his voice remained calm, but Steele sensed he struggled to suppress his rage.

"I don't know, Papa."

"You need to tell me, Thurgood. The truth will come out eventually, it always does." The phone receiver hung in the air, his finger ready to circle the rotary.

"I really don't know. We got split up." Submitting to the inevitable, shakes and sobs overwhelmed Steele. He couldn't speak anymore. Papa's face softened, he replaced the phone's handset and sat beside Steele.

"Let it flow, Thurgood. Emotions locked away will fester, someday erupting more violent and harmful. I need to know what happened, when you're ready, to be sure those boys are safe."

The release cleared Steele's chest, and he assembled the events for Papa, including Drew storming off, Chris's disappearance, the missing pistol, and the mystical shape above the creek. Again and as usual, Papa's practical advice proved correct.

"So, Drew should be home by now, and Chris is still out there."

"As far as I know, yes," Steele agreed.

Levi dialed Chris's house first, with no answer; tried Drew's and spoke with his mother, then tried Chris's again with the same result. "You're the first one home. None of the others are back yet, it seems."

"Thurgood, you're grounded for the entire summer, do not leave this house or yard unless I give you permission."

"But, the fair…" Steele trailed off. Complaining or protesting with Papa would lengthen the punishment.

"We'll see about working at the fair. That's it. Go to bed."

Pounding bangs rattled Steele from sleep, he pulled on shorts and a t-shirt, followed Papa to the front door. Two police officers, both women, stood somberly, light sun barely illuminating the horizon behind them, heavy clouds threatening a torrential downpour. Steele's head whirled as if he just stepped off the Spokane Spinner at the fair.

"Mr. Steele, this is Officer Crackle and I'm Officer Van der Waals. We need to speak with your so—," she paused, then offered, "with the young man behind you." Her eyes scanned the dried pink layer covering most of Steele's body. "May we come in?"

"Depends." Papa refused them entry, stepped out and closed the door.

Moments later Papa returned, the officers still outside.

BOYS' RECKONING
1987, June

"Thurgood, sit down. The officers brought sad, terrible news. Chris's father was shot in the night. Chris disappeared."

Steele didn't comprehend Papa's words, like Papa shouted nonsense through a pillow underwater. Steele repeated the words mechanically. "Chris's father was shot, and they can't find Chris?"

"Yes. I'm so sorry," Papa reached to hug Steele, who began quivering as the message seeped through.

"Ohmygod, no." Steele rejected the idea. Chris could never shoot anyone, but to shoot his father? No. When Chris's temper flared he became a firecracker, all noise and no substance; some Cheezey Oodles and cola brought him to normal. Hadn't Steele found empty Cheezey Oodles bags in Chris's trail?

"I'm bringing the officers inside. It's about to rain. When they come, you tell them exactly what you told me. Answer all their questions truthfully. They need full and complete information to solve this situation. But," he paused, "omit the part about seeing the ghost."

"Why skip the ghost?"

"I believe you, Thurgood. But not everyone will. They need the facts—and actually seeing the Fiddler has nothing to do with Chris. You said he disappeared before that time?"

"Yeah, I went looking for him and saw the foggy egg in the branches." Images of the dancing orb rushed through Steele's mind, for a moment he thought perhaps he had only dreamt it.

As Steele repeated the happenings for the police, Papa brewed coffee for them, then dialed a phone number without looking at the list taped to the wall beside the phone. The officers asked details about Troy, Darryl, the gun, Chris's anger, and whether Chris talked about harming his father. Just as Papa told him, he shared everything with Officers Crackle and Van der Waals, except the Fiddler. As Steele finished up Mr. Cooper knocked and Papa let him in.

"Officers, Darryl Cooper here dropped Thurgood off last night around 1:30."

Officer Crackle smiled gently Steele's direction. "Thank you, Thurgood. Be glad you're safe. I see your grandfather loves you like his own son. That's obvious to us." She gripped his wrists, oblivious to Steele's resentment at the sting of those words. The other officer led Barrel Darryl downstairs for his statement.

Several newspapers from Albany to Poughkeepsie covered the shooting and disappearance, with the Poughkeepsie Journal following until the story tapered off. The final article ran two weeks later, moved from the front-page to page six.

Search Off for Red Hook Boy Who Shot Father
July 12, 1987

James Christander, the Red Hook boy thought to have shot his father, remains at large, reports local and state law enforcement officials.

Mrs. Ruby Christander initially called 9-1-1 when the boy entered her bedroom brandishing a stolen firearm at around 2 AM on June 27 this year. Emergency operation recordings captured the boy yelling, "You cheating ****, Mom deserves better!" before allegedly firing one shot into his father's chest. Numerous sources confirmed Mr. Christander's multiple extramarital affairs.

Emergency room officials at Northern County Hospital pronounced Mr. Roy Christander dead on arrival.

The boy ran from the home, eluding search parties in the two week old manhunt.

Mr. Darryl Cooper, who found the boy miles from home the night before and whose gun James purportedly stole, led one search team. The weather frustrated the search, according to Mr. Cooper, who stated, "Them rains the day after he done shot his dad washed out any scent. My dog didn't find no trail neither. I still think he went back to them woods." Mr. Cooper's highly respected tracking skills previously assisted law enforcement in the 1979 search for a lost six year old, resulting in the girl's rescue from a centuries old well.

Law enforcement officials ended the search for James Christander yesterday, stating no leads remained in the investigation. The boy's two friends, who accompanied him that evening, remain shielded for comment at their guardians' requests. Anyone with new information should contact law enforcement officials.

J.S.
2000 Eight

Rosa deposited Steele at the house and headed to her shift at the bar. She agreed to return after work.

Steele inserted *New Adventures in Hi-Fi* in Papa's DVD player, an underappreciated gem of R.E.M.'s discography. Eclectic song stylings from country-tinged slow tempo contemplative musings to classic Mike/Michael intertwining voices filled this collection. The band explored phonic horizons and vocalized techniques including edgy spoken word and a guest appearance from a hauntingly subdued Patti Smith that balanced the rough edges of Stipe's maturing voice. Ah, Steele still fantasized that one day, somehow, he might cross paths with them to personally thank them for the inspiration through adolescence and beyond.

He attacked Papa's closet, those box stacks haunting him. The front stack held untouched shoes, unlaced and stuffed with balled white newsprint, unusual for Papa to hold items he never actually wore.

The back row revealed photos—old photos of buildings from the Dutch era, some labeled, some random. To date and place these photos would be time consuming, perhaps a project for a doctoral student's assistance, if locations could be identified at all. Another held old financial documents, tax returns long obsolete, and real estate records scrolled tightly, holding their shape independent of the disintegrated rubber bands clinging in shreds.

A box of portraits grabbed his attention. Like the photos of Dutch ruins, Papa's handwriting neatly captured some individuals, others left unmarked.

Steele recognized names from Papa's meticulous genealogical endeavors. Van Zyl, Staats, Steele, Halstead, Van der Kleij, Wooden, Stegenga, and Visser intersected; some surnames lost in the New World mixing of British and German immigrants in his paternal family stew. Few women appeared in the photos—those that did held infants or young children. A couple yellowed newsprint clippings emerged among the photos.

One image centered on a mustached gentleman holding a framed document featuring the Statue of Liberty, although the fine details of the paper behind the frame's glass seemed indecipherable. The gentleman beside him, also mustached, held a knife. Joep Stegenga and Jonathon Halstead, 1890, clearly written on the image's back.

Steele inspected the photo using Papa's magnifying assembly, as critical to Papa's survival in his last decade as a cup to hold water or a plate to carry food. He confirmed the image—the Statue of Liberty. Steele recalled the dedication occurred in 1886. The words Souvenir Programme, now legible with magnification, floated above her, with the word Souvenir curling down like a wave; spelling of the word programme with the extra M-E as still common in the late 19th century in the U.S.

The knife did not appear smooth in the photo, and Joep (or Jonathon) held it as if attempting to boast the etching on its blade; both men holding their artifacts between them, staring unemotionally stoic behind their mustaches.

This image likely documented a significant event in their lives, Steele speculated. Both names appeared on Papa's genealogy charts as residing between Staatsburg and Red Hook, and any trip to New York City would be a major undertaking in their era—even with the convenience of railroad, the cost of travel and lodging in the city erected barriers for most rural farmers.

The blade's blurred image remained frustratingly unclear under this pedestrian home magnifier. Steele required a stronger tool.

Instruments at the university's historical investigations lab might reveal the image's details more deeply. Could the knife that belonged to Joep Stegenga, whose initials he etched in himself, be the same knife Drew found in the woods? Or perhaps the blade belonged to Jacob, who by chance inherited Joep's initials and added the markings? Joep fathered three daughters and may have passed the tool to George Steele, Papa's father and Joep's son-in-law, who eventually inherited Joep's lands. Steele feared he would get mired in the quicksand of historical research when no conclusive evidence of provenance emerged, and put the knife aside for more investigation when the estate settled and he resumed his professional pursuit in academia.

Rosa arrived around 2:30 smelling of beer and cigarettes, showered, and slid into bed. Steele's overjoyous zeal prematurely teetered into disappointment, but the morning tangle of limbs and lips tottered into balance.

They tackled Papa's detritus all morning listening to a rotation of *Green* and *Out of Time*, *Green*'s hard edged guitar and politically tinged lyrics balanced with Out of Time's mandolin-soaked, whimsical songs. Steele chose to highlight the group's range for Rosa, who recognized only the pop hits *Stand* and *Losing My Religion*. If this relationship progressed as Steele yearned he would coach her to tolerate, if not appreciate, his musical obsession.

Their afternoon efforts targeted the garage, a snarled mound of Papa's gifts supporting each of Steele's passing adolescent interests, together with various tools and broken household appliances. Covered and buried beneath the layered jumble—and likely not functional—the 1966 Pontiac LeMans stood resolute, it's seventeen feet boasting stories long forgotten.

"Your Papa didn't drive?" Rosa inquired.

"He drove for many years, but not often. And not this. This belonged to Jacob." He waved his arm around as if dispersing a putrid smell. "Other than basic errands he rarely left the house. As I look back now, his reclusiveness diminished his prominence around the town. You've heard of the Red Hook Apple Festival and Parade?"

Rosa nodded, random strands of ebony hair framing her face.

"Well, Papa started that event. It's been about twenty years since he last went, but his pride never waned."

"You really loved him."

"I wonder what my career might have been if he hadn't showered me with stories of this region. I don't dwell in those hypotheticals, though, anymore. Papa ingrained a purposeful direction of living without regret in me—he always created a new analogy of regret to drill that notion. Without parents around I dwelled over the perceived gap in my life, and Papa just *knew*," Steele stressed the last word, "*knew* instinctively about my struggles of feeling so different from my friends."

"Tell me some of his analogies of regret." She tugged on a rusted snow blower, with well-rounded biceps pumping.

"Many revolved around apples, of course. Apple diseases. He'd spit off blue mold, scab, blister spot, gray mold, blights, mildew, rust, sooty blotch, leaf blotch, flyspeck and the rots."

"The rots?"

The way she tilted her head titillated Steele, he nearly lost the topic. "Um, like, crown rot, mucor rot, white rot, black rot, bitter rot, blossom rot, and probably more rots than I'll never remember. Such as 'Regret, a disease of the soul, like sooty blotch on Golden Delicious;

'Regret: the black rot of happiness;

'Blight in an orchard kills the fruit, like regret to the soul;

'Mold on the cider is like regret: bitterness consumes the sweetness of life."

Rosa shot one out, "Regret is acid on an orchid's roots." Her dark hair draped over her left shoulder as she bent to tug a foot pump from beneath a rusted chainsaw, a red spaghetti strap top struggling to prevent her breasts from freedom. Her burnt sienna skin glowed under soot and sweat; stirrings of round three for the day teased Steele.

She retrieved a box of newspaper clippings, silently reading while he dislodged a forgotten weed whacker, inanely chatting, "I'd like to invent a week whacker—some machine that can do all my work in an hour, leaving me time to nurture my passion."

Rosa remained engrossed in her discovery, barely nodding.

Steele rambled on regardless. "To build a functional seventeenth century living Dutch demonstration settlement, attract tourists from the region, educate and entertain, make a living while I'm at it. The week whacker slashes all the academic research for tenure to one hour."

"Steele, these newspaper clippings from the summer of 1987. Did you know this boy, James Christander? You would have been, what, fourteen, about his age?"

Papa organized the neatly clipped articles chronologically, about a dozen stories. He probably hid them from Steele, to protect him from knowing details about the murder investigation—Chris identified as the only suspect based on his mother's statements, fingerprints on the gun, and witnesses. Steele read them dispassionately, as he might while preliminarily reviewing historical documentation to formulate a research question. Droplets of information from Drew and other friends and neighbors trickled to Steele since *That Night* thirteen years ago, so the clippings revealed no new evidence—except that Papa kept them hidden. Rosa tried again, "Steele, what did you know about this?"

They remained in the garage for another hour, the R.E.M. discs long since finished, as Steele dove deep through the intricate details of *That Night* for her. Other than Papa and the police, only Drew heard this elaborate version, just after their punishments ended in the summer of 1987. Despite his valiant but futile attempts to suppress memories of *That Night* he vividly recounted each detail, recalling specifics such as Julia's name and how the Fiddler's apparition swallowed the branches without disturbing the leaves. Rosa listened patiently, never seeking a clarification, allowing him to pace the story in his measured cadence.

"So, no one heard from Chris again, even until now?"

"Not that I'm aware."

"And your friend Drew, from the bar, there's no more he knows?"

"We don't keep secrets from each other."

"I'm not convinced there isn't more to the story. More secrets someone holds. You're unsettled, cuffed to this personal narrative. Chris's disappearance still festers in that hole in your soul," she whispered. "You're a mess. My mess." Her eyes glanced downward and nimble fingers crawled up his thighs beneath his shorts.

BRIDGE
2000 Nine

"Will you come with me to the estate attorney tomorrow?" Steele impulsively uttered the question as her head rose and fell on the pillow of his chest.

Rosa hesitated. "That seems like your duty. I'd be intruding. I'm not family."

"We're together now," he countered, "you've peered deeper into me than I have explored in a long time. It may not appear so from the outside, but I'm unsteady. I put on a façade of control, but underneath, without Papa I'm stable as jelly on an octopus. I need you there to ground me."

Driving over the vast span of the Kingston-Rhinecliff Bridge, rising above the treetops and hills that surrender beneath the massive spread of the mile-wide waters, Steele's inner geek awoke, centering him in his comfort zone like a puppy on its mama's teats. "Did you know the Dutch called this Rio de Montaigne, before they named it Noortrivier? The Iroquois and Mohicans each used names in their languages, of course. Ironically the Dutch paid the Englishman, Henry Hudson, to explore this area and the British assigned his moniker to the river after gaining control of the region."

Rosa sliced through his diversion, "You're avoiding thoughts of this meeting, right? What are you afraid of?"

"I just, well, never mind." His inner geek insisted on bursting through the surface of thoughts continuously, but Steele suppressed the urge. "I'm not sure what to expect. Papa talked about days when the family owned lots of land, but not what happened to the land. Honestly, I have no idea what to expect from this meeting. Maybe Papa owed money, and I'll be instructed to settle his debts." He shrugged, grew quiet, focusing on Route 9W and Broadway towards Roundout, the classic brick three and four story buildings glowering in horrid pastels. Charles Dickens, Esq. owned the building housing his office, his name ornately calligraphed on a plaque near the entrance door.

His assistant escorted them to the office, warning them to call him Chuck and never—never—mention his namesake.

A portly, tall man in his mid-fifties, shiny cinnamon bald head with a neck like a giraffe, greeted them tepidly and motioned them to sit in the plush brown leather chairs straight out of a 1980s crime film. "This is unusual," Chuck skipped introductions, "these days I simply email the document to the beneficiary, and arrange a phone meeting to explore any open questions. However, the late Mr. Steele provided explicit instructions and conditions before we proceed. You are Thurgood Levi Steele, I presume?"

"Yes, and this is Rosa, my..." girlfriend? Never saying it aloud before, how awkward to pronounce it for the first time in the aseptic setting to the standoffish attorney.

"Friend," she suggested to Chuck with a pursed lipped smile, politely extending her arm to shake his hand.

"I'm sorry for your recent loss," Chuck offered mechanically. "The late Mr. Steele never provided a full explanation of why he structured his intentions this way, but I'll get to business. Mr. Steele stipulated that in order to claim your inheritance you must locate and bring two other individuals before me. Their names are Mr. Jacob Joep Steele and Ms. Marika Elizabeth Miller. I am not to provide any further assistance until that meeting. Do you know these individuals?"

Dumbfounded at the condition, Steele paused to collect his

thoughts. Why did Papa resurrect long forgotten people, strangers to him? Dead and buried from his life, forcing him to open their tomb. "These names, they're on my birth certificate, but I never met them."

Rosa interrupted the thorns and spears piercing Steele's brain, "Chuck, what if they're dead?"

"The will provides instructions for that event. Convincing documentation substantiating their death will suffice in lieu of the individuals; also if they are not physically able to travel we can make alternate arrangements for a location of the meeting."

Bloodlines continuing to trickle through Steele's mind and he blurted out, "What is the inheritance?"

"The late Mr. Steele's instructions are to detail the bequest at such time as all parties convene," he paused, "but I will state that he left substantial assets. And...," Chuck inserted another pregnant pause, "there is one more condition. According to the terms of his directive, you have only one week from notification to find them and bring them here. Until such time as all parties converge, the estate will remain in trust, under my care, per his wishes. You may, however, continue to occupy the house on Rimple Road, Mr. Steele."

"What happens if he can't bring them in one week?" Rosa probed curiously.

"I'm not permitted to divulge the contingency," Chuck stated, blinking awkwardly, "Good luck."

Too shell-shocked to drive, he passed the keys to Rosa once they reached the sidewalk. Rosa dropped them in her handbag, squeezed both his hands while drawing his eyes to hers. "Steele, I know that lady, Marika. There's no easy way to say this." She drew a breath before revealing. "She's married to my father. She raised me. She didn't give birth to me, but for all purposes she is my mother."

SOUTHWEST SMILES
1994

"The damn Raleigh Rainbow got a faulty drive shaft, it ain't safe, we gotta keep it shut down 'til the parts get in," Jake reported to Ranger.

"How long that gonna be?"

"It'll be delivered to Hartford next week."

"Thanks, Jake. Listen, I got somethin' I need you to do for us next year."

"Next year? For how long?"

"The whole season."

"What the hell you plannin', Ranger?" Jake leaned back in the chair, slipped a wad of chaw in his mouth for the legal high now that Ranger'd started random drug testing everyone.

"Need you to go undercover, be my inside man. Pretend you're just lookin' for a new circuit. They'll see that you know your shit. Here's the deal, Jake. You get to know the operation, management. Rumors flyin' through the association that Southwest Smiles Amusement's lookin' to expand and soak up other regional operators. Heard they've been eyein' us. I ain't gonna take that shit, wanna throw it back on them. They don't know you."

"They ain't gonna pay me crap."

"Don't worry, I'll make up the difference in pay. You ain't

gotta worry."

"What do you wanna know?" Despite the smoking, chew, and shouting his falsetto-sounding voice pierced over the rides' droning and hissing.

"How they treat their guys. Fair? Are they takin' advantage of the men? Are they lettin' others hopscotch along or do they book the whole damn show? What's the trainin' like for safety and mechanical? With the business changin' so much, we gotta treat people good to get 'em back. Learn it all, but play low. Start north with 'em, work south through October in Arizona. We'll meet up in Gibsonton for the cold weather break."

"What else is in it for me?"

"You know you're in line to take over the company. I'm gettin' older, someday I ain't gonna make the circuit no more. You got what it takes, and the balls to stand up to the cheats in this business. Still plenty of guys that'll rip us off from concessions to the genny. I seen it in you your first summer."

"I want the plan in writin'." Over twenty years, Jake trusted Ranger unquestioningly. His relatives, and any kids that might be floatin' out there, might jump in and want a piece of it, and Jake needed the law on his side of this deal.

"Done, son, done." Ranger and Jake shook hands, web meeting web and eye meeting eye as Levi taught Jake in a long-forgotten conversation.

Lions, monkeys, and warthogs swallowed the midway that summer. When a new, huge cartoon movie busted out, the games printed cash.

Southwest Smiles' rides needed more repairs and carnies treated guests better. Management noticed Jake's skill with wrenches better'n most the corndogs workin' their circuit. Still, years of loyalty counted over Jake's talent with tools and he grinded out the crap jobs they threw at him. It'd been years since he spent all season hands on, and the lower stress felt like a paid vacation.

Jake snuck calls to Ranger, lettin' him know these guys would mutiny with some of Ranger's low benefits levels. Ranger'd need to give more days off, and step up medical beyond the catastrophe policy; he'd need to stretch pay over the off-season too. Jake heard "they treat us right out here" more times than the winning bell in the water balloon race.

Wandering down the jungle-infested midway, jointees sagging from end-of-season weariness, his thoughts already nestled in Florida's west coast winter laziness and fishin' trips to Beer Can Island, Jake abruptly stopped. The stroller behind him crashed his heels and spilled cola on the sleeping toddler beneath her mid-size lion. Without hesitation he recognized Ka, ten yards away, beside the Tickle Train.

Her blonde hair now lighter and speckled with white, jowls defining themselves with onset of middle age, she carried distinguished, curvier proportions than her teenage self, even more attractive in her mid-thirties. Her head tilted slightly to the left, and her slim nose slanted downward at the tip, the trademarks he recalled during the infrequent moments his thoughts rewound to their passionate days. Despite the late season desert heat, faint memories of a spring breeze beside the Hudson tingled his skin, his head in her lap dreaming of his future. Would she remember him? Instinctively Jake's legs drew him to her, his focus drowned out the screeching, cola-soaked toddler and her raging parents. Ka guided an ebony-haired, brown skinned teen girl and two younger, lighter skinned girls through the bedlam of peak midway traffic.

"Ka, is that you?" She stiffened, only one person had ever called her by that name; long forgotten in her past of cold winters. The falsetto tone cemented his identity.

Hairs on her neck perked. "Go away. You don't exist to me." She remained with her back to Jake.

The teenage girl stepped between the carny and her twin sisters. "Mama, quien es este?"

"Un fantasma. Rosa, traer sus hermanas para el carrusel." The tall, older girl hesitatingly grabbed each girl's hand, Liza on the left and Inita on the right as always, leading the younger ones towards the KidZone's merry-go-round.

Marika inhaled, centered herself, rotated to see Jake, his oil stained overalls, muscled arms, face sun-browned and creased from his labors. Graying, curly hair thinning slightly with a shadowy widow's peak emerging; he's aged beyond the twenty or so years since she slipped out in the night leaving the three Steele men alone.

"Ka, I…" Jake trailed off, suddenly not sure he had anything to say.

Leading schools and students for years, she instinctively commanded the situation. With a practiced hand, she waved him off. "Jake, our words for each other died long ago. Just tell me, the boy?" Tears seeded the corners of her eyes, water in the desert; she blinked to banish them.

Jake stared at his grimy work boots; her dusty feet in leather strapped sandals, toenails painted a cotton candy blue.

"The boy, Jake. Is he…" Alive? Healthy? Strong? Smart? Maybe even—she dreaded to contemplate it—here with him? What did she need to know about the boy, the son she discarded; yet whom she intuited from time to time?

Jake shrugged, still looking at the ground. "I couldn't stay. Left just after you. Never been back home. Never seen him again."

Marika delicately touched Jake's forearm, fingertips grazing his fine hairs, a current sizzling along the underside of her arm; a montage of memories flooding this arid emotional landscape. She turned, following her daughters—flesh and blood daughters, emotional heirs of their unknown brother's affection—parting from Jake's callousness.

"Jake, what the hell you doin' with the locals? The Fresno Freefall needs lubin'. We still got two more days, then you do whatever the hell you want." Bells, buzzers, babies, bings, bursts, bangs, booms, and barks broke Jake's bubble. He trudged off, silently finishing Ranger's assigned exile.

Marika's forgotten phantom haunted her night. Carlos slept, oblivious of his wife's inner torture. Entombed grief powered open the stone covering its hollow, releasing violent torrents. Remorse's sunken weights walked the water's surface. Year after year passed, she never thought of the boy—convincing herself she truly rid her present of her demonic act.

Besides his life, she left behind only one item for the child. One message, sourced from confusion and passion and concern and revelation. His muddied and lasting truth. Sealed in wax, stamped with her thumbprint, a revelation.

In the Steele house, the key and knife rested atop the aged wax-sealed envelope bearing Marika's thumbprint.

THREE PUPS
2000 Ten

Astonished, Steele rode home mute, the usual fantastically scenic drive simply a blurred distraction. Rosa knew his mother—not just knew her; Marika rescued her, raised her, was mothered by her—mothered by his mother. Those scenarios he fantasized, torturing his mind with concocted infinite combinations of parental schemes—Rosa embodied his lost experiences. She pierced the thick silence.

"Steele, we're not related, not by blood. My father married Marika."

"But your half-sisters are my half-sisters—that's blood." Steele thought about their intimacy as people who share a parent. Is that what Rosa implied?

"There's no blood directly between us," she repeated.

"But, the woman who gave birth to me—then abandoned me—she disciplined you, taught you, joked with you, bought you gifts. We share a mother. And now we share a bed."

"Forget that. We have no genetic connection. She gifted you a life to live; she gifted me the opportunity to live my life in this country."

"She loves you; she abandoned and forgot me. I'm a mistake pissed into her toilet of time—from Marika and Jacob both."

"Steele, no." Rosa reached for his hand to soothe him; he

127

snatched it away.

"Let the past remain past. I don't need this inheritance. I'm a tenure track faculty member in a highly respected history department. I'll muster a decent life on my salary."

"Steele, your past runs deeper than Jacob and Marika. You told me of your family's prominence over generations. In my father's culture we honor all those that went before—our grandfathers and grandmothers, their grandfathers and grandmothers. To honor them is to honor yourself, and to honor your grandchildren. Our parents link us with the rich tapestry of ancestors who toiled and celebrated all life; we link our ancestors to all those yet to breathe the air, feel the sun, drink the water, consume the food of the earth. Even after generations of Catholicism we continue to cherish these ancient values."

Steele listened detachedly.

"Steele, you have to reconcile your past to embrace your future. Forgiving those who trespassed against you relieves you of your burden; someday perhaps Marika and Jacob will confront their actions—you can't alleviate them of their crosses." Rosa turned the car left towards Red Hook, down a thickly canopied road. "You'll walk with a lighter step, live more freely. Forgiveness is not a selfless act; forgiveness is selfish at its core."

"You sound like Papa now," he interjected with a forced grin.

"Forgiving others allows you to more fully embrace your true self. My father shared a story with me, and I'll share it with you; then my lecture is finished, mister professor.

"A mother coyote gave birth to three pups. She nursed the pups until they showed signs of independence. As the day they would leave approached, she told them of their test into adulthood. They would need to solve one problem.

"She dug three holes, each twice as deep as the pups. She nudged each one into a separate hole, buried them, and she ran into the wilderness.

"The first cub panicked, asking only why his mother would bury him alive, not attempting to dig himself out. He died within minutes.

"The second cub dug himself out, found his mother's scent,

and shadowed her until he thought she slept. When he attempted to nurse from her, she shredded him into pieces.

"The third cub tunneled out, ran the opposite direction from his mother's scent, and later fathered many litters of his own." As she stopped the vehicle in the driveway he caught her eyes, sparking a shift in his demeanor. Her expression both challenged and supported him.

"Steele, you now decide which type of pup you'll be."

UNRESOLVED UNCERTAINTY
2000 Eleven

Vibrations on the bedside table startled him awake, the phone's microbounces resembling the hyperactive Mexican jumping beans on the same table a couple decades earlier. Micheal, Mike, Bill, and Peter stared out from a 1987 Rolling Stone cover proclaiming R.E.M. America's Best Rock & Roll Band—before the majority of their seminal creative efforts graced the airwaves.

"Hallo," Steele intoned Papa's pronunciation.

"Dr. Steele, this is Dean Radowitz. Have I woken you?"

"No," he lied, shaky voice, then coughed to mask the lingering slumber, "just a bit of a cold."

"Dr. Steele, your bereavement leave terminates today. Please confirm you shall return to the classroom on Monday."

"Dean Radowitz, I planned to call later this morning. I had the opportunity to observe remnants of a foundation from circa 1665, with an extended kitchen along the eastern wall and likely additional enhancements approximately a century later. Although significant work will be required, this may provide critical evidence informing my hypothesis about the influence of Friesian—" his cadence escalated before she cut him short.

"Dr. Steele, that's a matter for another conversation. For the moment, urgent administrative matters must be addressed. Are you able to return next week?"

Taking a cue from her dry tone he adroitly responded, "Unfortunately matters of the estate remain unresolved. The attorney presented the final instructions, which necessitated additional time away."

"How much time?" the dean demanded.

"That's uncertain. Additional family members must be located, and convinced to return here to address…obligations."

"The university's policies may not allow for additional paid time off. I'll refer your situation to Human Resources for consideration. They will require a detailed written statement."

The phone went silent.

MAMA DON'T PREACH
1996

Rosa's restlessness stirred Marika's memories of leaving Red Hook, yearning for the ideal utopia in Colorado; Marika empathized to such a degree she envisioned herself travelling with no destination, rekindling her wanderlust. She coached Rosa to handle aggressive men, to frugally sustain herself, to listen to her body's desires and to respect the road. "Roads lead to places already explored. The views change from desert to mountain to city, you'll tingle with excitement for the wonders of this majestic planet—revel in the differences imagined beyond the next horizon. When the luster fades, you'll find yourself slightly wiser, yet largely the same as before and you'll look to the horizon to conquer that next place. Go. Go until your mind and heart agree to stop.

"And call us. Send letters to the girls. They're young, don't fade from their memories." And come back, she wanted to add, but suppressed it. Marika dwelled on abandoning her parents, never returning, never communicating; now reluctantly tolerating the karmic ache of being left behind.

SEE A HORSE ABOUT A MAN
2000 Twelve

Drew wandered into the hotel to occupy his customary seat, glanced at Rosa and muttered, "Usual, please." Grabbing a chilled glass she poured his beer, leaving a head a bartender in Amsterdam would approve. Not sure what, if anything, Drew knew about her and Steele, curiosity tempted her to draw him in conversation. Being only one of two customers, chatting with him would also pass time. Lacking the charisma of his friend, balding with a starter-kit paunch, his full red beard sparked up his otherwise dull appearance.

"Hey, ever hear the story of the ghost horse down near the river?" she asked to spark banter.

Drew's eyes shifted right, dredged his memory, he shook his head. "Seems there's a ghost story around every corner in Rhinebeck, but I don't remember the horse story," he lied.

"I've heard a couple versions. One features politicians, the other businessmen. In both versions two powerful men meet in this bar—back in its heydays, after the Civil War—and share drinks. Turns out they're both running schemes to defraud the U.S. government into overpaying for raw materials—some say lumber, others say cement—from around here for reconstruction efforts in the South." Rosa paused as a third customer, a slim lady in her mid-sixties she guessed, straight white hair pulled into a ponytail, entered through the door. After mixing a gin and tonic, triple lime, for her Rosa moved along with the narrative. "The guys realized their interests competed, and the debate heated up. They moved outside for a duel, near the train tracks, where a hitched horse stood illuminated by a half moon."

A motion from a gruffy guy with stringy hair and graying sideburns sidetracked her, she refilled his bottom shelf whiskey, and returned to Drew. "Anyhow, to shorten the story, they fired at each other; being drunk they missed, but one shot took down the horse. I've never seen it, but a couple times customers have asked me why there's a horse tied up near the tracks."

Always quick with his first round Drew's mug stood near empty. She refreshed it for him, "It's on me."

"Thanks," he raised it to toast her.

Rosa returned after checking on the other two patrons. "Your friend who came in last week, have you talked with him lately?"

Nodding, Drew said, "Yup. Sounds like you two hit it off. He needs a great lady, his last girlfriend soured him. They lasted about a year and a half, then she started dating a woman and walked over him like a doormat in a donut shop. Finally, she just stopped calling him and didn't take his calls. Please, he needs some kindness. Be gentle."

"Tell me about his parents. He's told me they left him as an infant."

"Honestly, I don't know much about them either. Same as you, they left him with his Papa."

"Know anything about his mother's family?"

"The Millers? Heard they moved away after his mother disappeared. Steele's mother didn't have any siblings. Don't think he ever met his grandparents on his mother's side." Rosa didn't recall Mama speaking much of her parents, never mentioned any brothers or sisters. She moved off to change the channel for the woman, mixed her a vodka and soda, triple lime; kept distance from Drew during his third and fourth rounds. When his shoulders dropped and his steps sent him askew down the men's room trail, she hoped he would open up about *That Night*.

"One more? My treat," she angled her face so the dim

lighting hit her cheekbones, glancing over her shoulder to him offering her contours in profile; a move she'd nicknamed Tip Turbo.

Drew half-nodded.

"Steele showed me the key and the knife. Said you found them in the woods somewhere. Did you ever try the key?"

All these years, Drew thought, and that key resurfaces. The door inside the cabin, the darkness beneath. There's a cliché, drunk and confessing to a bartender, he thought. But why not? Dark dreams of the key stalked his nights, images of drowned shadows enticing him down. End of June is coming, the dream will intensify, visit him nightly as in all the years since. Even after giving Steele the knife and key, the dream repeated. "Yeah," His speech slurred slightly, "under the cabing, I mean cabin. It unlocked the cellar door."

"What cabin?"

"The bunned, I mean burned one. In the woods. We went there all the time grown up. Growing up. Steele and me." And Chris. Since *That Night*, Drew never spoke Chris's name to anyone besides Steele. "Steele knows."

"What's there?" Rosa intentionally found Drew's unfocused, bloodshot eyes.

"What's where?" Too much beer, he realized. Drew left the second freebie barely touched.

"Under the cabin. Did you see anything?"

"Too dark. Really dark. Nightmare dark. Couldn't see anything."

"Have you gone back again?"

"Not my place. Steele's family ownged—owned—the land. Used to. Didn't want to trespass much." The ponytailed lady down the counter scribbled the air with an imaginary pen, and Rosa printed off her bill. Sideburns man mimicked the lady.

As Rosa cashed out the other two customers, Drew zigzagged to the men's room again. Neither noticed Steele as he entered.

Steele admired the jukebox's alternative music catalogue sample: Nirvana, Mazzy Star, Hole, Pixies, Smashing Pumpkins, Beck,

Weezer, Jane's Addiction, Sonic Youth. Like 1995 arrived and the owner stopped adding new music. He injected a bill, picked R.E.M.'s *Everybody Hurts* from *Automatic for the People*. Stipe's falsetto vocals wafted through the fusty air.

Rosa spun, not masking her delight in seeing him. Steele resisted whisking Rosa to waltz to its three beat rhythm— R.E.M.'s most soulful, sorrow-filled ballad padded in friendship's phoenix power. Drew rounded the corner as Stipe reminded Steele to seek solace in his friend.

Steele embraced Drew, Drew mumbled to him. "Go to the old burned cabin. The key workds. I mean, works. On the ground, near the old stove, there's a metal door. I found it *That Night*." Drew smelled of light ale and sorrow.

Steele stood, momentarily dumbfounded. "Why didn't you tell me before?"

Drew shrugged. "Dunno. Didn't think it important. Used to be your family's land, might be somethin' there for you. Damn key's a nightmare, keeps coming back. Glad you have it now." Drew started towards the door, bounced off the pool table into a chair, bald head and red beard resembling the orange-stripped thirteen ball.

"Drive him home," Rosa ordered Steele.

Drew waved him off. "No, no, I'll walk. I need to see a horse about a man," winking towards Rosa, he turned left out the door towards the river instead of right towards his apartment.

Talking over one another their voices clashed. Rosa edged him out, "I'm closing now. We can't stay."

"Can we go to your room?"

She balked, their sibling/not sibling debate replaying itself in her mind.

"To talk," he clarified.

Just as bedraggled as the whole building, peeling deer print wallpaper and sagging drapes adorned the neglected space. Her speck of a room barely contained a footpath to squeeze around the bed. Not sure where he wanted to sit, he took the straight back chair, its wicker seat fraying on the rear edge.

"Rosa, I'm terribly conflicted," Steele spoke deliberately, selecting words for precision as he would for a research journal article, "my heart intertwines with yours, I've never felt as unified with any soul the way we've connected; making love with you is truly love making."

"But," she blurted, expectantly.

"But, my rational mind won't let me. Not yet. Until I find Marika, talk with her, sort out this situation. Not for the money, or whatever Papa left, but to reconnect the disconnected.

"For years I invented scenarios of living with my parents, to be like most of the kids that grew up around me. I fantasized about them cheering at my baseball games or teaching me to ride a bike or grounding me for not eating peas. I conjured trivial and significant events throughout childhood and adolescence. At my high school graduation I yearned that magically one or both might appear, somehow learning of my accomplishment and seeking to be a part of that day. Papa's attention soothed the ache, but I still wanted them."

Rosa settled onto the bed, just within arm's reach.

Steele continued. "Eventually I learned to accept my experiences as unique, creating who I have become. Not to crave for what could have been, what should have been. Those wasted efforts of yearning dragged me into depths of despair. I thought I'd overcome that torment," he paused, eyeing the crooked dresser drawer.

"And now it's returned. I suppose I never really buried those thoughts—and now they need to be confronted, as you challenged me on the way back from the lawyer's office. What is that Zen belief, we exist only in relation to other people, other creatures, and the planet?" Steele crossed his legs knee over knee and shook his dangling foot.

"I'm stumbling. My Dean called, inquiring when I'll return. I pushed her off, telling her only of legal technicalities delaying the process that need my attention. My bereavement leave finished, I'm now into personal leave, and only have a few days left. After that is unpaid leave, which I cannot afford. I need to figure all this out quickly." He suppressed the impulse to reach for her hand.

"I've bottomed out before. College shocked me. Arbor College, even though it's right here, was an entirely new experience. More like progressive arts education, much beyond liberal arts. With freedoms beyond any I could imagine, I ventured into hard drugs, sexual experimentation; essentially lost all the values Papa instilled in me. Dragged me down, way down, where I remained most of my year right out of high school. The drugs magnified, intensified all my regrets. I lost my scholarship with atrocious grades and moved back in with Papa.

"Papa steered me back to school though. I signed up at the community college, which took some of my advanced placement credits from high school. I felt the instructors took interest in me—me—and my future. The instructors sparked my desire to learn, really for the first time in my life." Steele uncrossed his legs, ran his fingers through his curls.

Rosa shifted, propping herself up on one elbow.

"Mr. Taplin taught history backwards. We started the class with the events of the day—the U.S. invasion of Kuwait repelling Iraq's forces. Mr. Taplin reversed the events for us, revealing Iraq's motivation after being defeated by Iran. Through the semester we traced events to the turn of the 20th century, and I became an apostle. I couldn't learn enough, needing to trace back and back more." Steele shifted on the uncomfortable chair tenderly, careful not to stress it and fall through.

"Is that the beginning of history, or the beginning of the historian?" Rosa joked.

He acknowledged her humor with a forced smirk. "I began to understand why Papa read so many books, his desire for knowledge now infected me. And I needed to learn about history." Steele pictured laying next to her, tearing loose her turquoise tank top.

Steele refocused, becoming more difficult the longer he lingered close to her. "The gaps in history fascinated me in particular. Why hadn't we learned the Native American perspective on white encroachment? How did the Italian domination of the mafia affect later waves of migrants? How did imposition of U.S. centric values deconstruct Puerto Rican customs?" His enthusiasm intensified with each question.

"On breaks I read from Papa's historical collection, relating it to my adventures in the nearby woods, tramping over—and ruining—historical evidence that continues to resonate in this region. Place names around here took strong significance for me.

"And history is stories. Simple. I'm a glorified storyteller, a well-educated story addict. Who, where, what, how, why—and importantly—who's telling the story." Rosa stretched fully on the sagging bed, fluffing a pillow, hair spread like a mermaid. Conflicted thoughts revisited Steele. Sister? Not sister? He envisioned her riding him the day before, black hair whipping wildly.

He refocused, reluctantly. "Ironically, the gaps in my personal story faded—or I grew preoccupied with other peoples' stories. My sole goal became to obtain a tenure track position to continue researching holes in history, bringing me to where I am now professionally. History continues to ignite me, sparking my passion to learn and learn. But."

He stopped the narrative, slid off the chair and beside her on the bed. "You've woken my heart. I can't deny that," he paused, "Rosa, will you...."

Her body stiffened, breath quickened, pulse spiked.

"Will you...take me to Marika?"

Her tensions released.

"Tomorrow?"

"Yes."

Pulling her close, thoughts of being siblings—or not—joined the ghost horse of the railroad tracks.

LEAVING NEW YORK
2000 Thirteen

Just before leaving he grabbed the wax-sealed envelope, his full names *Thurgood Levi Steele* delicately penned from corner to corner; vines of flowers flowing from the stamp area through the words and into the lower left quadrant. He sensed the time to open it might be approaching.

From Albany they connected in Washington, D.C, then Dallas for a regional jet into Las Cruces. Rosa drove through her home terrain, allowing Steele to survey the foreign landscape; a harsh juxtaposition to the Hudson Valley's lush greenery where life seemingly pushed through each roadway crack. Here plants struggled to declare their existence.

Steele lost himself in the expanse, feeling immersed in R.E.M.'s *New Adventures in Hi-Fi* cover photo, supposedly taken by a band member through a tour bus window during the *Monster* tour. The vast openness absorbed him: he circled above as a bird of prey, glimmered with infinite stars, crawled the scorching sands as a scorpion, blew as arid winds, stood sentry as a cactus, whispered secrets of lost societies, flowered after rain's gift, shivered with a winter snow, scoured for dead flesh as a vulture, nestled in a squirrel's burrow, tracked a desert hare as a coyote, and ran from a coyote as a jackrabbit.

The police siren's *WHURRP WHURRP* startled Steele awake.

"License and registration, ma'am."

"Umm, it's a rental, sir," Rosa looked flustered as she dug around her purse for a license. Steele reached for the rental documents under his name.

"Where you two headed?"

Steele offered, "Sightseeing, sir. Taking a break from New York."

Inspecting the documents, the officer questioned Rosa, "Ma'am, this is an ID, not a valid driver's license. Please provide your operator's license."

She caught Steele's eye, desperation and apology seeping through.

"Officer Rodriquez, I'm not feeling well, I asked her to drive; I felt we'd be safer. Flying makes me lightheaded and dizzy, on top of my cold." Steele concocted.

"Wait here," the officer returned to his vehicle.

Steele quizzed Rosa with a slight squint of eyes, tilt of head, and flick of one hand.

"No license," she admitted. "I've never owned a car, only learned to drive so my friends could party. Easy to drive at night with empty roads." She gazed beyond Steele into the desert, hands trembling beneath the steering wheel.

"Ma'am, please step out of the car," he ordered. "I'm taking you into custody."

"For what?" Steele shot at the officer impulsively, then attempted again more respectfully. "I'm sorry, what are the charges?"

Officer Rodriguez volleyed a severe glance at Steele but addressed Rosa. "Ma'am, radar clocked you at 85 miles per hour in a work zone, you're operating a vehicle without a valid license, the names on your ID hit a match with Immigration and Naturalization Services, and possible possession of false identification." Then to Steele, "sir, are you capable of safely operating this vehicle? If not, I'll call for it to be impounded and order a taxi to take you to your destination."

Steele nodded, disbelief knotting his stomach as the cop cuffed Rosa and led her to the patrol car, a steadfast stone face shielding her emotions.

"She'll be held at the Deming Police Department until first hearing tomorrow morning," Officer Rodriguez offered to Steele.

"Find them at 224 East Cherry Street," Rosa shouted before being stuffed into the police cruiser's austere back seat.

Steele drove, barely registering traffic with his concentration ping-ponging between Rosa and Marika. At Deming's outskirts he stopped at Milly's on Wheelies, with severely sweaty servers skating lopsided burgers and wilted shakes to customers. The server placed the paperboard tray on his lap and he asked for directions to Cherry Street. Pointing with his fist, the twenty-something server's strength could have flipped the car with one arm, Steele suspected. He grunted a set of turns that sounded more like fruit salad ingredients than navigation instructions—Orange Road to Peach Path to Melon Way.

Rosa will need a lawyer, but how to find one in this tiny town, and after hours? And for any immigration issues, Marika and her husband should have answers. Doubt crept into Steele about Rosa's story. A false ID? Could he trust anything she shared?

A square town with square streets and low, rigidly rectangular homes painted the same sun-soaked color as the gravel and roads, after several ninety degree turns Steele crawled into the semi-circular driveway. He pondered his opening. To knock on the door, announce himself as Marika's discarded son, and that her beloved adopted daughter sat imprisoned a mile away seemed ludicrous; like an apparition materializing and giving her the exact time of her death. Not an approach to endear him to her.

Imagined infinite times since early in his adolescence, the imminent reunion would materialize in Deming's reality. Embracing him, together they would create an oasis of tears in this torrid landscape. He'd tower over her, her head in his sternum, sobbing with joy of eviscerated years, her voice quavering, repeating *my boy, my boy, my boy*. They'd gain composure, stare at each other in amazement, scrutinizing the face now consuming each other's vision to validate the resemblances in curves of their ears, pointed chins, slender noses, thin lips. Yes, of course; so strikingly similar there would be no doubt the son found his birth mother. No doubt.

But perhaps a small variation in the chain of events might establish credibility. Would he be able even to speak, let alone adjust the truth? Lying *That Night* to Papa taught him a simple lie steps down the path to regret; yet the point of his journey to New Mexico was to exorcise him of regret's anchor.

Heart pounding, sweat collecting everywhere it could, he emerged from the car. He'd already caught a glimpse of a teenage girl peeking out the window. Better to start somehow than stall now. Ringing the bell doubts swelled and he fleetingly hoped no one would answer. He could begin to forget this nonsense, tuck his past away and reinvigorate his aggressive research agenda towards tenure.

Two teenage girls cracked open the door, one with hair dyed the color of the surrounding soil, the other with a nearly shaved head and pierced lip. The nearly bald one asked, "Yes?"

"Um, yes, I'm, um," he stumbled as they started to narrow the gap in the door at his hesitation, "I'm a friend of Rosa's. We just arrived in town, but she's in trouble. Can I speak to your parents?"

The shave-headed girl nodded, the other mumbled. The door closed, latched. It promptly unlatched, with a muscled middle-aged man emerging, closing the door behind him. They shook hands firmly, web to web.

Steele started again stiffly and with more confidence. "Hello, I'm a friend of Rosa's. She wanted to surprise you with a visit, but she's had a problem."

"What's your name?"

How should he answer? With such distinct names he couldn't use any without possibly outing himself. "Drew," he lied hypocritically, "Drew Christander."

"She never mentioned nobody when we last talked. Never talked about no visit. You sure you found the right place?"

"Yes, sir. Garcia is her family name. She was born in Mexico, lived with her grandmother, and came here when you—um, her father—married an American woman," *my mother*, he thought, "and she has two half sisters, Inez and Elizabet."

Carlos held a steadfast look, not revealing his reaction. "What trouble is she in?"

He remembered saying problem, not trouble, but this wasn't the time to dwell on word choice. "The police, here in Deming. They arrested her for an immigration issue—and speeding, and driving without a license."

Carlos hurried, invited Steele into the home, then disappeared out the back door barking at the girls to cook for their guest.

The vivid colors of the sitting room captivated Steele. Bold red throws and blankets printed in broad bands with horned animal silhouettes cloaked the couches and chairs, a herd frozen in fierce sunset. Sagging light strings at random intervals traced hand-drawn posters of saddled turquoise horses, violet hills, glowing auburn castles; a corner shelf from floor to the low ceiling spewed clocks, Marian icons, Spanish novels, a calabash, elementary school teaching guides. And family photos. This home's bright cheeriness countered the spectrum of gray to beige of his upbringing; Papa's one burgundy armchair needled the color edge of their decor.

Spanglish snippets floated from the kitchen, pans on a metal stovetop clanging unhappily. The pierced-lip sister delivered lime soda and a glass with three ice cubes, avoiding eye contact, obviously annoyed by this nuisance visitor.

Sitting next to the cabinet, Steele examined framed photos arranged like tree rings with older memories in the back. In front, a couple of posed school pictures, perhaps two or three years old, featured the girls. Another one, Carlos, twins thigh high, and an elderly woman with her weather-worn brow, an adobe structure in the background. A thin film of dust fogged a photo of Rosa and the twins, Rosa about fifteen or sixteen, each biting into cotton candy, a merry-go-round twirling behind; in a plastic sunflower-yellow frame. Further back in the shelf, a gray toned photo of a blonde, longhaired hippie girl, ecstatically waving her arms, oblivious of being photographed; several shaggy men lounging in the grass around her.

Trembling, Steele poured soda into the glass, using both hands to steady the bottle.

"Why you shakin' like that?" the other girl asked, placing Maria cookies on the table. Steele didn't hear her walk in.

"It's been a long day. I'm St...," he caught himself about to say his real name, and she recognized his hesitation, "still feeling the road."

"I'm Liza," she tossed her ecru hair back with a shake, "how you know Rosa?"

"We're friends. Met in Upstate New York, through her work."

"Just friends? Why would she come all this way with a *just friend*? She been away for, like, five years, hardly ever calls and never emails or nothin'. Then you just show up and say she's in jail? Somethin's up."

Steele hadn't thought through his cover up. Panic kicked off another round of perspiration.

"Liza, ven aquí!" Inez shouted from the kitchen.

"You hidin' somethin'," Liza accused him as she turned the corner.

Carlos entered the house from the front, a policewoman behind him. Instinctively Steele rose.

"I'm Officer Schmidt. Sit down, I just have a few questions," she towered over Carlos, a light sprinkle of gray hair mixed in her brown bun, tattooed eyebrows angled like boomerangs.

"How is Rosa, is she okay?"

Carlos answered. "She's fine, as fine as can be in a small town jail."

"Relax sir, just a few questions and I'll be going." Officer Schmidt spoke softly, intimately. "Now, your names please." One eyebrow angled like an arrowhead.

"Hold on. What is this for?" Steele struggled to procrastinate, not wishing to reveal his real name. Not yet.

"Just want to verify some facts. You can call a lawyer, if you wish, but we might be able to, um, dispense the matter more simply," she stated in a matter of fact tone, layered with sultry intrigue.

Steele reluctantly decided to return to honesty, channeling Papa's philosophy; tension reigning in his stomach. Lying never served him well. And lying to an officer would bury him beneath more complications. "Thurgood Steele."

Carlos shot Steele a disdainful glare. "You told me your name was Drew, when we was outside," Carlos challenged him.

"To some people. Thurgood Levi Steele is my legal name." Saying that truth aloud assuaged his nerves.

"And how do you know Ms. Garcia?"

She's my sister? My lover? Both? "Friends. We met at her workplace in New York and decided to take a trip out here on a whim." Not the whole truth, but no falsehood either, Steele comforted himself.

"What do you know about her immigration status?" Her angular eyebrows imitated a mosh pit crowd as she spoke, distracting Steele.

"Just that she came here as a small child." This is meandering into bigger issues, Steele thought, perking his heckles. "Officer, with all respect, I should not continue without a lawyer for her, or me, present."

Carlos stood sharply. "Excuse us," he shot towards the officer and motioned to Steele to follow him out the back door firing rapid instructions in Spanish to the twins as they passed.

In the bare courtyard a crumbling fence surrounded an area no bigger than a two-car garage, yellowing cream-colored plastic Adirondack chairs squeezed into the lengthening shade beside crusty pet food bowls. Carlos' biceps and pecs bulged, firmly squeezed in his tight yellow t-shirt, emblazoned with a local restaurant's name, The Rickety Shack.

"You show up here, tell me my daughter is in jail, lie to me about your name, while my other daughters serve you drinks and cook for you. That's not respect." Carlos's voice remained low volume, bristling with intensity as his eyes narrowed like coin slots.

"Rosita hardly never calls, never come back since she ran off.

You hiding something. You tell me so we can clear this up with the police. I can get her out soon if you pay the ticket fines. They haven't filed any immigration paperwork yet. Tell me what you want. The truth." His muscles twitched, a vein beside his temple surfaced, right fist clenched instinctively.

Steele exhaled, rolled his eyes upward for strength, returned his gaze to Carlos's eyes. "I didn't intend to bring trouble. I came to find Marika."

Carlos flinched, eyes narrowed more. "For what? What you want now with Maria?"

Steele refused to reveal everything, despite the rising tension. "It's personal, very personal. I can only tell her."

"She's out. Campaigning. She'll be back later."

"Campaigning for what?"

"Never mind. I don't trust you. You give me the money for the ticket. My Rosita will explain to me. She ain't no liar."

Steele passed cash to Carlos, hoping to buy goodwill along with clearing the fines.

Carlos returned an hour after Steele finished the exquisite pork machacas Inez and Liza prepared, expertly balancing the spices and limiting the heat level. The house cooled significantly after sunset, when the girls opened all doors and windows, allowing the dry breeze to blow through and the neighbor's polka-laced beats to dance in. Steele began to doze just before the front door creaked open. Carlos entered alone. Steele wished Rosa would materialize. How would he broach the topic of being an abandoned child of Carlos's wife?

"The fines are paid, and the immigration cleared. They're considering charges for using false identification until the morning, so she's staying the night," Carlos peered at Steele, drilling a hole in Steele's chest.

"Did you see her?" Steele asked, hoping for a crumb of positive news.

"Yes."

"What did she say?"

"Enough," Carlos shuffled down the short corridor and

shouted over his shoulder, "Maria's on the way. Don't go nowhere."

Go where, Steele puzzled. Come reunification, come mother.

Jetlagged from the long travel day and stuffed from two full meals within hours, Steele drifted off before Carlos reappeared in his guard's uniform for a night shift.

Pounding at the front door startled Steele, his shirt clinging at a large wet spot near his shoulder. Liza bounded across the room, wearing a black pleather-laced corset, black lipstick, and a black pleather skirt as wide as a hand towel; her hair tucked into a black cotton beret, several strands like pillars beside her face. Instinctively Steele quizzed her, "where are you going?"

"Screw you," she countered with teen arrogance, and slammed the screen door closed.

Steele stood, immediately became dizzy and bent over to rush blood into his head. Inez, in a red tank top and white shorts, turned the corner, finding him doubled over, "Anything wrong?"

Returning upright, he shook his head, "Just dizzy, happens sometimes." They sat down, him back in the armchair and her on the sofa's end beside him.

"So, why you wanna talk with Mama?" Steele noticed a birthmark on her upper arm, shaped like Florida—nearly identical to his birthmark in the same place. His gaze lingered.

"Why you looking here? You want some?" Her hands framed her breasts pushing them up, head rounding half moon, lips tightened. "You already goin' with my sister, so why not, right? Same family, yeah? Aah-ite," Inez reached for Steele's crotch as the screen door groaned and Marika materialized, formally dressed in an indigo pantsuit, graying blonde hair in a pixie cut.

Marika flung her purse with laser aim, the handbag crashing into Steele's head, spewing makeup and credit cards and mints and receipts. Inez vaulted, dashed behind her mother, shrinking into a timid posture. "Get the hell out of my house! Now!" She lunged forward and grabbed Steele's arm, adrenaline decimating her exhaustion, Inez tugged his other arm shoving him towards the door like a slingshot.

Steele, sensing a warm trickle along his left eye, desperately shouted, "Wait! I'm Thurgood, Thurgood Levi Steele! Your son!"

DOIN' WHATYA DO
1992, February

"Why you keep doin' this, Jake?" Ranger prodded.

"Doin' what? Workin'? What the hell am I gonna do, sit on my ass and drink beer? I'd last half a day. Gotta keep movin', can't sit still," Jake flicked ash to the ground as they huddled around a small fire. Florida's chilly winter nights needed this warmth, even near Tampa.

"You ain't supposed to flick it like a cigarette. Let it build up, it'll fall when ready." Ranger pulled on his Ybor City Corona, a treat from Jake for Ranger's birthday. The embers canoed, Ranger pulled a stick from the fire to even the burn. "We've been haulin' together for goin' on twenty years. You gotta have a reason to stick with it this long, Jake"

"Don't know what else I'd do. I like fixin' the rides, roamin' the country, change of towns week to week."

"You gotta have somethin' deeper than that. For me it's kin. My family's been in the business for a century, I keep it goin' for them. Got plenty of cash in the bank, don't need no more if I live another sixty-three years. It's in my blood is all." Ranger puffed from the cigar, rollin' it in his fingers. "But you, you comin' from apple farmin', family goin' back there forever. Jus' like me and the carnivals."

Jake drew on his cigar, a heavy, hand rolled Kick Arse

150

Torpedo. A couple drags and flyin' already. "Guess it's the kids. Seein' the young ones grinnin' on the rides, blue mouths suckin' down cotton candy; and the older ones shittin' their short shorts on the thrill rides. We make folks happy, forget their worries for a time, livin' and enjoyin' the moment. Thousands and thousands of kids each day. Really don't git much better than this." He pulled another deep mouthful of blue-gray smoke.

Ranger shuffled live oak logs in the fire.

Thoughts swirled deep from the toxins, stirring up sediment from Jake's past. He confessed with his shrill voice, "You know I left that boy when I joined up with the circuit. Never seen him again. This work is kinda like for him. What I done to him."

Ranger let the ash fall from his penny colored roll. Jake's ash fell too. Silence seemed the right response.

"By now he's finishin' high school, if that's his ballyhoo. Might be in college. Who knows. I ain't done nothin' for him. Now I'm makin' a place for all these other kids to enjoy—prob'ly millions by now."

What he done for all these other kids won't never make up for what he done to his boy, Ranger thought. "You think you'll ever find him?"

"Nope. Don't want to. Leavin's prob'ly the best gift I'd ever 'im. I ain't cut out to be no one's daddy. " The fire collapsed, sparking a brief flare up as the logs settled again, a bitter gust of wind licked them like a kid on an ice cream cone. The weather forecast called for a wet, stormy beginning to the Florida State Fair, as happens nearly every year, but time-honored superstitions kept the forecast unspoken. "Just hope he's doin' what makes him happy," Jake closed the topic with Ranger.

Jake tossed uneasily in his cot. Out west, in New Mexico, after seeing Ka with her girls, he drowned in the quicksand of regret. A boy with curly blonde hair, a dense green fog surrounding him, stepped out of a cactus and crept towards Jake; the thin boy slightly bent one knee, raised his right hand to his forehead to begin the sign of the cross, whispered *"Father,"* dropped the hand to his upper stomach, mouthed, *"Son,"* angled the hand to his left shoulder, murmured, *"Broken,"* completed the tradition at his right shoulder, delicately stretched the syllables and lingered, *"Ssssssspppiiiiiiiiiiirrrrrrrrrrriiiiiiiiiittt,"* the boy's body lifted off the ground, the boy raised his arms horizontally, lengthening and thickening into mature cacti arms, the glow darkening to olive green; his legs united into one cactus trunk sinking into the sand; his curls straightened into spines and face morphed into the cactus. The monstrosity collapsed forward wrapping Jake in a jade gloom, sucking his lungs of air. He shattered the suffocating murk in javelin kicks, waking on the floor, cot upended, catching his breath. *What the fuck was that?*

MARK OF BIRTH
2000 Fourteen

Marika froze, the commotion vanquished by Steele's abrupt revelation. Steele searched his mother's eyes for a trace or sign. Nothing.

Steele dropped his arms from their grasps, turned to Inez, and drew back the Kelly green polo sleeve covering his upper arm. "Look, my birthmark is nearly identical to yours, same place." Inez glanced at her arm as if she'd never seen her birthmark, then to his bicep.

Marika struggled for the closest chair. She swayed, disbelief-infused confusion knocking her off balance. "Inez, agua." She gripped her upper arm too, hidden beneath her tailored blazer and silk blouse. "I've feared this day."

"Feared?" Steele asked, bewildered.

"Nervous, anxious, apprehensive. Hoped I'd have made my celestial transition before you could locate me." Disbelief and disappointment infused her tone.

"You never wanted to meet me?" Steele felt like a car with a deflated tire veering into a gulley.

"No. Yes. No," she vacillated.

Inez handed the glass to her mother. "¿Quieres que me vaya, mamá?"

"No, stay, Inez. Sit. I've hidden this—him—long enough

153

from you and Liza and your father. From myself. I've anguished untold nights puzzling over his fate. Whether he survived, who raised him. There's nothing I gave him in this life. I simply vanished, abandoned him and my family."

Yes, Steele thought, anticipating the revelation in this cluttered living room.

"Mamá, Rosa le trajo aquí," Inez threw gas on Marika's smoldering fire, not fully believing Steele's excuse of examining the birthmark rather than her chest.

"¿Mi Rosita? But, how? I...," Marika trailed off, staring vacantly again at Steele, "How? What? No. This is too much. Nothing fits."

"Yes, Rosa led me here. Your Rosa Maria Garcia." My Rosa too, he thought; but that would send Marika into cardiac arrest. Later, hopefully much, much later, she would learn that angle—although his romanticized plans for this moment thus far went as smoothly as the time he belched the alphabet at communion in mass after Chris challenged him in a dare.

Inez tossed a propane tank onto the blaze. "But Rosa's in the Deming jail, thanks to him."

Wobbly, Marika rose, balanced herself against the walls down the hall, silently shutting her bedroom door, and fainted in her pantsuit.

"You can't just waltz in here, throw a bomb on her like that!" Inez lashed at Steele.

"You were throwing me out, it's the only way I could stop you," he shrugged, perturbed. "I'm going to a hotel."

"No, you ain't. What you did ain't kosher, but we's family. And we aren't done. Sleep on the couch."

The creaking door woke Steele from an edgy sleep that ultimately overtook him about when roosters began crowing. Carlos entered, followed by Rosa.

"Welcome home," Steele mumbled groggily.

"This place looks the same as when I left, Papi," Rosa nostalgically rubbed a throw cover featuring elk silhouettes between her thumb and forefinger. "Looks smaller, though, like

I've gone through Alice's tunnel," she paused. "Are the girls awake yet? I'm dying to see them."

"They'll wake up around noon, Rosita. I'm going to rest. You and your friend need to catch up." Carlos disappeared down the hallway, not glancing Steele's direction.

Rosa pecked Steele on the cheek, and he flinched away. "Please, not here, not yet. It's complicated."

"Whatever." She stepped across the tiny sitting room, seeing the purse's shrapnel scattered around the floor, then noticed the dried dribble of blood on Steele's face. "What happened here? Did you meet Mamá? Inez? Liza?"

Steele detailed lying about his name, Carlos' reaction to her being jailed, Liza's indifference, Inez's birthmark matching with his and her sexual advance, and the crowning fiasco of his long awaited meeting with Marika torpedoed by Inez. "It's been like ordering a bottle of expensive wine, anticipating the flavors' complexity, but the waiter slamming the bottle over my head."

Rosa winked at him, "Welcome to the family, mi amor."

ABORTING MOTHERHOOD
2000 Fifteen

Marika emerged as Rosa delivered jet fuel coffee, corn cakes and spit-fire scrambled eggs for Steele. Mother and daughter embraced and wept cheerfully, ecstatic to reunite, volleying rapid staccato Spanish. Despite Steele's four years of high school Spanish, his speaking ability encompassed one phrase: ¿dónde está el baño? A pragmatic phrase, but he'd never understand a response.

Steele followed the gist of their conversation while savoring breakfast: Seattle, Boise, Detroit, Madison, New York, barman, and seemingly random English words sprinkled among the Spanish. Rosa's travels and life since leaving home; when the subject shifted to Inez and Liza their pitches slowed, voices softened, melancholy seeped into the room. Marika barely acknowledged Steele's presence; Rosa darting approving glimpses as Steele cleared his food. Marika removed the utensils, allowing Rosa space to whisper with Steele.

"What do you want to tell her?"

"Everything, and nothing. Last night, before Inez tossed a grenade into the conversation, Marika began revealing why she abandoned me. That's what I want to hear."

"'Hear, hold, hurl, heal,'" Steele recited, "another of Papa's ingots."

"What?"

"First, hear out their side. Let them talk. Ask questions, understand. Listen from a distance. Visualize their story as a globe—see the definition of land and water emerge. Probe for clarification.

"Next, hold onto their view until you understand completely—you don't need to agree or accept it, simply clutch the globe in your hands. Rotate it upside down—put Antarctica at the top, flip your vision.

"Hurl the globe into space as you release the tensions in your mind. See the planet in orbit, settled into a delicate balance around the sun. Occasional meteors pummel the planet, causing temporary distress that settles—and heals. Heals back to the natural rhythm and balance in the universe.

"Master this process to heal your internal universe—the infinite space of emotions, thoughts, sensations, desires, and experiences that meld into the singular self."

"Your Papa taught you some unique guidance," Rosa's rosy lips repeated the sequence. Hear, hold, hurl, heal.

Facing the past ten days, Steele began to understand how much Papa revealed to him. And how much he didn't—or couldn't—or wouldn't.

Marika returned with a plastic pitcher of sweet, cool pineapple-infused water and three mismatched glasses, placing the largest in front of Steele, a keepsake pint glass from an educational conference in 1994. She set the tone authoritatively. "You've come to find your past, Thurgood?"

Rosa stood to leave, Marika waved her down. "No, stay. You're my daughter, listen. I've hidden my past far too long from you—and them," she waved toward the back of the house.

A fist-sized gizzard swelled in Steele's neck. "Yes. Papa told me nearly nothing about you."

"Well, it's similar to a story you've likely heard before—a generic TV variety drama. But in real life.

"I was a pregnant teenager, and I refused the thought of aborting the fetus; at the time I would not harm any living creature, leave alone the one inside me.

157

"I couldn't take care of you. I was too young, too focused on leaving that place. Too focused on myself. I hoped and trusted Jacob would be able to raise you."

Steele interrupted. "He left too, not long after you."

Marika flashed to the encounter with Jake at the fair years earlier, how he'd grown broader and matured, sun-worn creases witness to his life outdoors. "Yeah, I know. Who, I mean, how were you raised?"

The dour weight of forced abandonment began to surface in Steele again. "Papa. Levi raised me."

"Oh…," she paused; it seemed to Steele that he tapped an emotional flare. "Anyhow, before getting pregnant I'd fixated on commune living, this in the early 70s after all. My older sister had moved west in 1970. I adored her—modeled myself after her." She leaned over to pour from the pitcher sweating, hand lightly shaking. "So, being pregnant with a baby—you—ruined my utopian dreams."

Steele felt incensed with her crass tone, as if she spoke of the stench of a rotting carcass.

"For a while I tried. I desperately wanted to love you. It's what a mother should do. The more I tried, the more I resented you for the burden of diapers, feeding, bathing; even though Jacob helped a little, when he wasn't drunk or high.

"My animosity intensified, and I began scheming of how to harm the baby. Or myself. I'd imagine the baby slipping below water in a bath; or rolling off the bed during a nap. I snapped one day, hovering a pillow above your small body, actually covered your face for what felt like eternity." Tears welled at the corner of her eyes. "Your little legs kicked and arms flailed. Then, well, you may not believe this next part, but this is the actual truth.

"Your body exuded a glowing jade-colored fog, like green steam off a boiling pot of water. A dense fog though, vapor but not vapor; hard like an impenetrable egg shell. The fog surrounded your tiny body and repelled the pillow.

"The haze lifted me next—not my physical body, but my spirit, my soul, my essence. The cloud felt icy, the dark unending cold of winter. I hovered over that scene, utter disbelief that my hands attempted to murder my baby."

A chill crawled over Steele's skin, his mother nearly killed him? A defenseless infant? Suddenly his decades' long obsession of blame on this woman turned to a blessing that she fled. And that fog she described felt familiar, almost like the mist *That Night*. The orb as real to him as his right foot.

"Postpartum depression?" Rosa interjected, breaking Steele from his tangential thoughts.

"In part, yes. We'd call it that now; back then it was taboo to not love your child. But I stewed in crushed dreams, teenage hormones, and banishment from my parents' house. That glowing green fog cleared my vision, I knew at that moment I needed to escape; it would be the best option for me," for the first time she found Steele's green eyes across the living room, "and for you."

Steele's scholar's ear analyzed the evidence for cross-references with the tidbits Papa told him; suppressing his emotions until Marika revealed all facts, cocooning in his comfort zone. Steele sipped the pineapple water, the day's growing heat parching his throat, and glanced at the photos in the corner. He caught Rosa's eye, she wore a quizzical expression. He realized his narrow lips formed a circle like a guppy and his eyes widened resembling a contact lens ad, his default look when detached from the situation.

"From New York I hitched rides to Boulder, finding the commune lifestyle I thought I wanted. The glory of shared work, shared resources, shared beds; but this turned out to be the early waning days of the hippies, and the commune lasted only a year or so before the early pioneers ventured off to sell insurance. The settlement folded, and I drifted into Mexico to learn Spanish. I imagine Rosa shared what she knows from there?"

Rosa's and Steele's eyes linked fleetingly, long enough for Marika to confirm complexities beyond platonic friendship. Steele wished to ask about her family—his maternal grandparents, the sister Marika mentioned, to begin deciphering the lines of Marika's globe.

Steele's hesitation allowed Marika to steer. "What do you really want? Just to meet me? If so, mission accomplished. My hunches tell me there's more. And my hunches are usually right."

Steele drew a breath, glanced again at Rosa, who avoided him this time. "Yes, there's more. So much more. Levi passed away," Steele paused, expecting a statement of sympathy, and continued when none came, "and his will stipulated a meeting of sorts before his intentions would be disclosed. You're among the three people required to attend."

Marika retracted, straightening her posture upright, dropping the throw blanket's fraying edge she'd twirled as she talked. "Never."

"And the other person?" Rosa prodded.

"The other is Jacob Steele," he sheepishly revealed.

"When apples grow in this damn desert." Finality permeated Marika's words and tone.

"But Mama—" Rosa began to implore.

"Levi deserves to be dead. I'm grateful he raised you—but what other choice did he have after all that happened?" she shouted, saliva flying and her face turning ruby, a tad lighter than the brilliant crimson blankets circling the room.

Rosa launched into a Spanish torrent completely beyond Steele's comprehension. Marika moved to leave, Rosa blocked her path to the kitchen. Marika aimed for the front door, Rosa pivoted ahead of her again. Marika turned for the hallway to the bedrooms, shoved Rosa aside, slammed the bedroom door and dove next to Carlos, shuddering as she relived that darkest, buried moment in the cabin.

FILCHED
2000 Sixteen

"There's trouble out west, Jake. Don't know how long it'll take me to git it straight'n'd out. I need ya to run the show for a while." Ranger pivoted in the maroon leather office chair, desiccated along the seat edges like a fish losing scales. "Money's not addin' up, someone's oach'n me. Might be the jointees all goin' south; might be the cash office; might be Pickle Fred swingin' the whole thing. He's not takin' much to me after I bought out Lonesome Mary."

"I'll go. Could use a change," Jake offered.

"I'll be back in a week, two at most, sure as a fly returns to a horse's ass. No, you're the only one what can handle these fudgepackers. What's that word? Finesse. You always persuade 'em to our side somehow, like a suede mallet." Ranger launched into another lingering coughing fit, like a generator sputtering after its fuel's drained. "Breathin' too much diesel exhaust and dust, son. I'm goin' on a mornin' flight from Louisville, you stay here. Keep the carnies in line."

"Showmen, these days."

"Show me my ass. They's carnies. Always'll be so long as I'm around."

His pistons are seized on this trip, Jake figured from Ranger's sucked in lips. With the Scranton Screamer failing a surprise inspection, Jake headed through the midway's flood of vacantly smiling yellow square plushes. Since Ranger bought out the Southwest Smiles he's snipped and argued all day long. Jake couldn't figure out what touched off his moods no more. Used to be a washed out stand was the only trigger, now seemed everything ignited him to a rage.

The sandpaper in Jake's throat sparked his own coughing spell, and he decided — again — to quit smokin'. Once he'd gone two years without a cigarette, cigar, or weed; then spent the night with that gypsy girl in Delaware — or South Carolina — or Tennessee — whatever. She and her 'sister' passed a pipe of lord-knows-what. Visions of carousel horses grazing, pastures of elephant ears and corn dogs flicked reality to a dumpster with them two. Next morning a lipstick ring round his balls and a t-shirt from Bud's Guns-N-Drugs in Suds, South Carolina is all he found; they'd cinched his clothes, shoes, cash, and wallet.

This time quittin' would be for real.

Prob'ly.

Some day.

Passing a candy apple concession, Jake remembered Levi pointing it out at the fair one year. "That's an abomination, son. They use Red Delicious for those things. Just about any other supermarket variety like Empires, Paula Red, or Gala and you wouldn't want to hide the bold, complex flavors under burnt sugar. But if they're going to use any variety, best to use the worst, I suppose."

Wonder what the old man would make of the apples now? Coated in chocolate and sprinkles; caramel and peanuts; dark chocolate and pretzels; white chocolate and coconut; caramel with toffee and pecans. Seems they just randomly roll apples in candy store leftovers and sell them for six bucks each. Damn insane, these prices. Figurin' in rent, electric and water hook-ups, percentage of their gross, and fixin' up arrangements with local health inspectors, six bucks an apple just about covered the basics. Since Ranger'd signed him on as minority owner at forty-nine percent, about two bucks of the six went between Jake and

Ranger.

Bet the old man never saw that much cash for just one damn apple.

Tiny details around the operation spooked up old memories of the old man. Roasting peanuts conjured up Levi in his chair, reading a goddamned book, dipping into a bowl of peanuts, shakin' em to take off the red skins. Scent of dairy cows at a rural stand and the names Joep Stegenga and Jonathon Halstead floated by in Levi's voice, boasting of their award-winning cheddar business. The monkey grinder's organ flashed to the cabin's stove. A scent of pizza and Jake glimpsed his father across a wobbly table at Mr. D's, Levi a giant towering above him, rattling off about some European goat herder that became a saint for castrated men.

The most vivid flashes brought Jake alongside Levi at the cabin. A branch swaying in the breeze, and Jake could almost smell Levi's sweat as they hacked trees for the cabin's walls. Jake heard Levi's grunts echoing in the ride jocks while assemblin' rides. A sharp snap from a slammed trailer door and Jake jumped as the cabin's cellar door crashed closed, temporarily deafening him from the forest's birds and hum of wind in leaves, *illillilli* drifting in sight, whatever the hell that meant.

Jake flinched at metal on metal clanging for almost two weeks. On those blessed nights between stands, when vehicles remained parked and packed, he enjoyed his cradle of warm slumber. Other nights ground his nerves to filaments. Why now were these memories snapping back?

Edgy, exhausted, and overwhelmed, Ranger's announcement about flying west poured water in Jake's gas tank. He'd coped with stress through cigarettes and whiskey, but that wasn't enough. He rounded the Country Coaster, the last wooden roller coaster still makin' the circuit, searchin' for Eddie Tang. Eddie massaged the circuit hookups from Florida to Maine for weed—one of his many talents with locals from cops to inspectors to prostitutes, best advance man they'd found since the seventies.

Eddie'd say each government rep is like beans in the chili—good at the start, rotten as a fart.

"Got any ganja, Eddie?"

Eddie's thin, bloodshot eyes answered Jake before he spoke. "Thought you gave it up, boss."

"Mostly," he chirped, "just need a little. Lot's droppin' all at once."

Eddie disappeared behind the genny, dropped a bag between its tires, circled the front and found Jake in a camping chair. Jake bent doubled over, hands muffling his ears.

"Dude, you okay?" He shook Jake. "Man, you lookin' like cow shit in a horse's hoof."

Jake creaked upright, motioned Eddie off with a half wave, leaving a bill in the cup holder. Jake mumbled to Eddie, the generator drowning Jake's whine like a rock in a lake. Jake hobbled away, stumbling over cables like a drunk clown.

Gotta figure out these flashbacks. Not like he went to war in Vietnam or nothin', he thought. Maybe it's got somethin' to do with the old man—he's gotta be around sev'ty now, thereabouts. Ol' codger probably choked on an apple core and gone to his saints' and sinners' orchard in the sky.

Or I'm losin' my mind, he feared.

MI MAMA, SU MAMA
2000 Seventeen

"This is all horribly wrong. What should we do now?" Steele disappointedly asked Rosa.

"I have an idea. The girls will be key. Let's get them on our side, after all they just gained a brother. In Mexico we say *a los amigos uno los escoge; los parientes son a huevo*—loosely meaning you choose your friends, but family is yours from birth. Their obligation is to help you."

"Their family is their parents and you, I'm a stranger to them," Steele rebutted.

"No no no," she repeated shaking her head, "Why build an obstacle? Their Mama is your Mama too. And don't worry about the girls, I'll take care of them. Here's your part. Take Papi to play pool, buy him beer and burgers. He won't admit it, but his weaknesses are American staples—even American football. Talk about history—he knows Mexican history, dig into that with him. Bring him home drunk, he's a giddy drunk, and you know I've seen all kinds of drunks." Her smile captured dawn's optimism, her gold-tinged skin radiant from the indirect light. He leaned into her for a kiss of desperation's lust, losing himself in primal impulse, her hand sliding inside his shorts from the bottom.

Liza, back from a night of partying, entered quietly through the back door of the kitchen, unlike its chattering front door cousin; while Inez emerged from the hallway at the same moment Rosa pawed Steele.

Rosa's hand worked slow motion when Steele noticed Inez in the doorway.

"Rosa," Liza indignantly peeped from the kitchen opening, "this your novio?"

Rosa withdrew, Steele turning flaccid, scarlet cheeked, flustered, and embarrassed.

"Novio, no," Inez countered. "Liza, Steele es our brother," spitting out the last word like a bitter seed.

"¿Que? No. No, no, no." Liza's contorted face revealed her confusion.

"Mama told me last night, this guy's her son. She's hidden this from us for all these years."

"Rosa, you yanking his pito, no? Our brother's dick, in Mama's casa? He your brother too, no?" Liza and Inez ripped into machine gun Spanish, firing at Rosa from two directions, pointing at Steele's groin, pumping hands up and down, cutting Rosa's words off. Their heads whorled, voices strengthened, arms flailed as the twins shot insults and exasperations at Rosa; Rosa defending herself from the verbal assault on two fronts.

Vibrations of chaotic shrieking woke Carlos and Marika. They scrambled to the cramped living room. Steele remained mute and seated, not understanding a word yet fully comprehending. Betrayal. Disbelief. Rage. Hostility.

All his fault.

Was this crumbling domestic fragility really of his making? Marika's suppressed secret would reveal itself one day, Steele reasoned. He, the secret, drove to the house in the flesh—he could no longer be burdened with the weight of her closeted past. Steele dismissed the roiling conflict as not of his creation—Marika's long-buried actions set up this clash.

Rising at a stalagmite's pace, he stepped over the coffee table, head bent to one side from the low ceiling, spreading his arms until silence reigned.

The feuding family grew silent.

Steele projected his classroom voice regardless of the tight room. "For my entire lifetime—twenty-seven years—I've lived without a mother. Fragments of her life floated to me from rumors and scraps of evidence. She was as real as my imagination allowed. Some days this phantom floated like an angel adoring me; other days she'd strike me with shoes and belts. Just fantasy, an adolescent boy's projections to fill the void she created.

"But you," making eye contact with Rosa, Inez, and Liza, "this same mother raised you since you were the youngest of children. Was she a perfect mother for you? I don't know. I don't really care. You've each been with her, you have real memories where I created fiction." He paused for that to take hold.

Marika slouched, dropped into a chair, and supported her head as Steele revealed his truths.

"Memories of birthdays and carnivals; punishments and fights; family trips. I'm envious of the breadth of those experiences. But I don't hold grudges. There's no ill wishes in my heart for any of you."

He fixed his azure eyes on Rosa. "Call it luck or God's will or the universe's divine intentions or fate, but Rosa and I found each other. We connected on a deeply spiritual level, that quickly became a physical and emotional attraction."

Steele stepped down from the table, motioned for everyone to take a seat as he remained standing.

"Shortly after you left," his gaze cemented on Marika, "Jacob abandoned me too. Papa raised me, never placing any blame on you or Jacob. Only attributing the circumstances to him, and how he raised Jacob. But Papa's gone now, too.

"In all these years I couldn't ask you for anything. I had no way to contact you.

"Through the universe's manipulation, I've finally found you, and I have one simple request. That you return to New York, attend a reading of Papa's final wishes. Then we can reconcile our pasts to open our futures."

The family focused on Marika, her leaded head sunk deeply in her hands, hair splayed randomly over her fingers, still and mute as a statue.

Carlos spoke first. "What's in it for you?"

Rosa answered, "The lawyer said there is a substantial inheritance. Steele doesn't know any more, Papi."

"At one point his family held huge tracts of land, but his Papa sold it, I think," Marika whispered, dredging up stale details. She spotted the wax-sealed envelope under the table, Thurgood Levi Steele in her own youthful penmanship.

"Before yesterday I floated alone in this mass of humanity, a historian unbound by relations. I want to close that chapter of my life. Now I've found family," Steele emphasized this last word, swirling like fine cider on his tongue. "Sisters. A mother. Whatever inheritance I might receive I will share."

"Or not." Carlos suspiciously questioned.

Marika bent forward, tenderly lifting the envelope, establishing that the seal remained intact. To Steele she confirmed, "You've never read this?"

"Never."

She held the envelope between both hands, solemnly, respectfully. "I'll go," she acquiesced, "on two conditions. First, Jacob must be there. Second, I want to read this for you with him there. Rosa will keep it until then." She passed it to Rosa.

The envelope with the deepest of Marika's suppressed memories.

The envelope with the revelation that would crumble Steele's remaining pillar of truth.

Now all in the hands of her son's lover, her eldest daughter.

HOPE
2000 Eighteen

Forming a crescent around the computer at the Memorial Library on Gold Way, Inez's card let them access the Internet. Steele doubted this simple screen with only a search box on a white background would be of any use.

"That looks too simple. There's nothing else on this web site?" Steele questioned, even the name sounded like something he'd do in private with no girlfriend. In his judgment this new search engine would soon disappear like those before it, something else popping up again next year.

"It uses complex algorithms based on word choice, what other people entered, and the popularity of what people click on. The trick is trying different combinations of keywords." Rosa and Steele shrugged as Inez entered *Jacob Levi Steele carnival fair* in several configurations and synonyms. Her vision tunneled while her fingers danced on the keyboard and pupils yo-yoed up and down the screen. "Got it, I think," she announced.

"You think? You're not sure?" Steele doubted.

Indignant, Inez scrawled *Ranger Rides and Steele Shows, Inc.* on a rough-cut eighth scrap paper in jagged lettering, along with a phone number. "It's only as good as the information it combs through," she huffed. "And there's plenty of details you don't have. Does this guy still work as a carny? Is he alive? Where does he have a house? Does he have other children? Maybe if you knew more I could target it better."

The kiln of the afternoon festered with the sidewalk radiating heat, the library's sunbaked brick walls beside them, and the intense solar rays; not an ounce of shade or pound of cloud in sight. Steele's sweat evaporated before it formed droplets, his lungs drying like a neglected sponge.

Barely able to discern the numbers on his cell phone's two tone screen in the glare, he tapped out the sequence Inez scrawled, dreading the long distance fees, roaming fees, service fees, and half dozen taxes that would inflate his bill.

"Ranger Rides," the uninterested female voice announced, a grinding sound in the background muffling her words. Steele wondered why she omitted the *Steele Shows* part of the company name.

"Um, yeah, can I talk with Jacob Steele?"

"Who?" she mumbled.

He enunciated more clearly, the mobile connection dropping syllables, "JAY cob Steele."

"Oh, Jake. He ain't around. Won't be back in Florida 'til Halloween," she explained like someone swatting a gnat with a beer can.

"Where can I find him?" Steele probed.

"Whose askin'?"

Who should he say? "Someone from his past, long long ago."

"Name please, and number. I'll get a message to him. Might take a couple days though."

Steele ended the call. After all, one doesn't 'hang up' any longer. "No luck," he reported to Rosa.

"What'd she say?" Rosa asked.

"To leave a message, and it would be a few days before he gets it. We all need to be in Kingston in four days."

"You didn't give any details. Think, Steele. Did she deny him?"

Steele shook his head, his curls bouncing after his neck stopped twisting.

"So, he still works there. It's a carnival company. This is

carnival season. He's apparently on the road somewhere. Trick is to find out where. You studied well enough to earn a Ph.D., but they didn't teach you common sense?" Rosa stripped the phone from his hand and mashed the numbers Inez scribbled.

"Hello, dear, I have a shipment for Mr. Steele, but the delivery instructions are unclear. Can you help? I need to know where to send them for tomorrow." Rosa intoned a passable Tennessean accent. "Instructions says he's need'n these parts ASAP, we just finished machinin' them. Customers first, you know," she paused, listening, "um-hmm...Taylor County Fair, Campbellsville, Kentucky. Got it. I'm sendin' a driver direct. We'll get it rollin' now. Thanks, doll."

Steele sheepishly accepted his phone from Rosa, hoping his blushing was indistinguishable from his sun-reddened cheeks. "I'll drive back to Las Cruces," he dictated.

Leaving enough cash for Rosa and Marika to fly to New York, Steele drove east on I-10 alone.

As the desolate landscape blurred past, Steele recalled a conversation with Drew the summer after they finished high school, four years after Chris disappeared. They'd decided to ride mountain bikes down to the river rather than drive, neither trusting Drew's 1981 Mercury Topaz. Each year around the anniversary of *That Night* they ventured out somewhere together, silently remembering Chris; mourning the void that bound them together.

Steele reached into his backpack, offered Cheezey Oodles to Drew. Drew waved off the snacks. He didn't get how Steele could eat those, too reminiscent of Chris; Steele brought them in honor of their lost friend. Steele's indifference to reminders of Chris irked Drew.

"Did you hear his family's moving?" Drew asked Steele, avoiding Chris's name, Steele noticed.

"Yeah, to Iowa or one of those I-states," Steele answered disinterestedly.

The vast river hurried quietly south, eager to join the Atlantic. Chris's shadow settled beside them.

"Drew, you think they'll ever find him?"

Drew shrugged. "No one's looking anymore. He's mostly been forgotten. Why do you want to talk about *That Night* as if it happened on a TV show?"

Steele ignored his friend's question. "What do you think happened to him?"

"I don't know could be lots of things maybe he made it to the city, found a way to survive there. I don't wanna talk about it anymore. Let's talk about something else. Anything else."

Steele plucked a stone from the ground, tossing it into the suds of the water's shallow edge. "I don't think he's alive. It's just a feeling I get whenever I think about him. I want to be wrong, of course."

They each retreated inward, lyrics to R.E.M.'s new song *Low* dragging through Steele's inner conversation. The misty lyrics touched Steele, as if written just for him at this moment of reflection, a flow of loneliness and interdependence and highs and lows of friends.

With no wind, and minimal bird calls at midday, the river's hushed gurgling and slight tidal lapping provided the afternoon's soundtrack. The friends exchanged few additional words, deeply lost in memories of *That Night*, each feuding regret's demons at what they could have done differently to stop Chris from killing his own father and vanishing with no trace.

In that quiet afternoon Steele recalled Papa's belief that even fallen apple trees offer multiple uses for the living—from firewood to whittling to mulch chips to the simple beauty of watching them slowly decay, merging with the earth to enrich new growth. Steele did not understand how Chris's likely death could possibly enhance his own life—if that's what Papa was trying to teach him.

Steele cracked the silence, "Papa talks about how dead—."

"DON'T GO THERE!" Drew roared in his non-stop trail of words, "I'M DAMN TIRED OF THIS CHRIS IS GONE HE'S DEAD we're not gonna bring him back DROP IT don't talk about him anymore!" He withered...and erupted again. "If I hadn't left you two *That Night* maybe he'd still be here now maybe I would have stayed awake at the bridge so he wouldn't have left on his own…maybe I could have called his parents. Maybe I could have stopped him from getting so angry but I wimped out I just gave up on you two. It's my fault he's gone, Steele. Just STOP STOP! NO MORE!" Tears burst from Drew as if a rain shower without clouds, he seized his bike and savagely peddled up the trail, the incline of no consequence to his strength.

Neither noticed the half-eaten bag of Cheezey Oodles shifted six feet behind them, into the weeds, despite the still air.

As Steele approached the airport exit, he reasoned Drew had finally found peace after *That Night*, that time and maturity mollified the misplaced guilt that trailed Drew through high school. Passing off the key and the knife to Steele alleviated any remnants of those irrational thoughts, he hoped for his friend's peace of mind. After that outburst at the river, and until Steele broached *That Night* recently, they skirted the incident. The knife seemed to be a keepsake, possibly from his ancestors' observation of the Statue of Liberty's dedication. But the key…the key…. He touched it dangling on his neck.

His pocket vibrated just as he slotted the car in the rental lot. Damn mobile phone becoming a growing nuisance, now he could be reached anywhere.

"Hello Dean Radowitz," he faked gladness to her.

"Doctor Steele, you've exhausted your leave days. You've become incommunicado. Unless you have a valid explanation, with evidence from an external authority, I'm afraid the university must begin processing your termination," she explained, as if teaching a three-year-old that seven follows six.

"No, please Dean. The family matter is much more complex than I presumed. The estate demands—"

She cut him short. "You are immediately suspended without pay for vacating your responsibilities to the students, colleagues, and institution. Unless you file a written explanation within forty-eight hours, termination proceedings will commence. Do you understand, Doctor?"

"Yes, Dean." He admitted defeat.

"Very well." The line went silent.

Not even a dial tone on this damned device, he thought.

He hesitantly began drafting a memo on the plane, frustrated by the subtle politics of his university's administrative apparatus. But sleep wrapped its seductive cocoon around him on both flights.

Reaching Lexington near midnight, all rental car companies remained shuttered until Tuesday morning. A bloodshot Ethiopian taxi driver with decaying teeth dropped him at a third rate hotel run by Indian immigrants besides the Little Havana restaurant on the outskirts of America's Horse Capital of the World.

Steele peeled down the blankets to inspect the sheets for stray hairs and stains from momentary acts of pleasure. Breathing the room's air reminded him of his bout with walking pneumonia, each breath saturated with a phlegmy dampness. The air circulator grudgingly whirred, wishing it might return to China.

What did he feel for Rosa? Had common ties to Marika woven their spiritual connections, some supernatural force quilting unity into their paths that they mistook for carnal passion? Her insights into his motivations astounded him, as if she intuited the emotional landscape of his essential being. She challenged him to face long suppressed fears buried under the sediment of time. Without her prodding he might have returned to his staid pursuit of knowledge for knowledge's sake and foregone Papa's final fickle directive to assemble his descendants.

But history must circle back into itself.

The niggling secret no historian would utter aloud: history contained one story arc, with different players and varying timelines. Migrations of peoples, separation, and loss; victors enjoying spoils of self-determination and triumph. Triumph, the byproduct of suppression and exploitation. Until the suppressed and exploited struggled for justice through upheaval, becoming victors.

Rosa entered his life like a tooth in an infant's mouth. Was he drawn to her to fill the void opened by Papa's passing? His stomach fluttered even now thinking of her. The image of how she angled her head slightly left when listening to him speak vanquished the neglect of this motel room. The tingle of her finger tracing his spine, imbued the sanctity of their union. Her ancient eyes, portals to his universe.

He embraced his truth for Rosa.

Love.

Sleepless in the pitiful room, fully clothed on top of the covers, Steele reflected on Marika. Who was Marika, really, to him? A parent? Not in the sense of his upbringing. Just the vehicle of his birth into the world? After seeing her in the flesh he felt no more attachment than if she birthed him in surrogate. Her reactions resembled indignation and aggression rather than the compassion and tenderness of his imagination. He didn't blame her for harboring resentment of him now, dropping on her life like a chunk of frozen airplane waste; throwing her normalcy into utter bedlam in less than twenty-four hours. His fanciful maternal bond evaporated like water from the kiddie pool in their barren backyard.

Or, succumbing to his love for Rosa, perhaps this line of reasoning served to distance him from Marika so as to legitimize his relationship with Rosa? They couldn't share a mother and be lovers, too. Could they?

Or, perhaps reckoning reality with Marika simply stripped off another layer of silt from the shipwreck of his soul. This woman abandoned him intentionally and scornfully. She confessed to attempting to murder him as an infant. She harbored absolutely no regret. He could not go backwards, only forwards.

Except, of course, while on thrill rides at the county fair designed to go both directions.

The memo begging for his job remained unwritten.

***

Steele drifted into an unsettled sleep, the altered reality of tangible dreams so vivid he woke up drenched from impossibly acrobatic sex with Rosa. By the time he dozed again and awoke the clock blinked at eight-thirty. Steele triangulated with his phone, the clock twenty-three minutes slow. Maybe cell phones have some redeeming qualities, he thought. With the Taylor County Fair opening at ten, he rushed out the room.

Limp pastries with condensation droplets in cellophane wrappers and translucent coffee suggested the owners acknowledged the offer of a continental breakfast—but which continent Steele wondered. He nabbed a local newspaper for reports and schedules of the county fair. Bollywood music floated from a dusty CD player in the corner.

The front page featured a controversial landscape installment at the town's funeral home, with opponents claiming orange flowering shrubs represented flames of hell, clamoring for the business to be boycotted. This served as news in Campbellsville, Steele gathered. The fourth generation owners, having just buried the third generation owners, claimed the Butterfly Milkweed and Orange Coneflower attracted wildlife to enliven the atmosphere and would not be removed, "come Hell or high-water," quoting Carl O. Campbell, the Forth (sic).

A full page spread on the fair languished at page eight. Today would be the final day in town. Nearly imperceptible print confirmed thrills and family entertainment was provided by Ranger Rides & Steele Shows, Inc. A nervous flutter crawled across Steele's stomach. Or hunger pangs.

"What brings you to town?" the owner asks, introducing himself as Rajesh, his double-u dropping as a single v. Steele noticed his unusually flat face, as if being smushed on glass.

"Just visiting. I'm heading to the fair."

"You taking your children with you?" Rajesh's with sounding like vit.

"No."

"You showing animals?" Sounding closer to shoving animals.

"No."

"You going for what, then?" *Vot, ten,* Rajesh pronounced. Always fascinated with accented English articulations, Steele could listen to him for hours if not under time's weight.

"Um, some research. Personal stuff."

Rajesh surveyed the six-car parking lot absent any guest vehicle. "You have a car?"

"No, I need to get a rental back at the airport."

"No, no. You rent my car. Thirty dollars for the day. Just bring back full."

Steele took up the offer for its time saving convenience.

Five minutes later Steele accepted the keys from Rajesh, Rajesh walking to the minivan with Steele. Rajesh's three children waited inside, his oldest child, a daughter of about sixteen, wearing an R.E.M. *Man on the Moon* t-shirt.

"What's this?" Steele asked, bewildered.

"They going to the fair too. Last day is cheapest day for rides, you see." Rajesh answered, as if explaining shadows to a toddler discovering them for the first time.

"But—," Steele began to protest.

"I promised them last week. No worries," *vorries,* as Rajesh verbalized. "You bring them back tonight, eat dinner with us. Yes?"

"But, you still want me to pay?"

Rajesh shook his head side to side, which Steele mistakenly interpreted as no.

Chauffeuring a stranger's children didn't quite coincide with his plans, yet his entire life veered off rail since Papa transitioned. For the free car and time savings, why not also help this guy out? An authentic Indian meal would be a satisfying reward for any inconvenience.

"Chandni, you take care of your brothers, yes?" Rajesh confirmed as he turned inside.

"Sidd, buckle your seat belt! Dhruv, stop poking Sidd! Guys, stop! Behave. Or I'll tell Daddy. Sidd, I said buckle the seat belt. It's too dangerous to stay without the belt." Chandni's one-sided nagging persisted until the boys grew bored of disrespecting her and ventured into an invented hand game. For Steele's entertainment she narrated Sidd's school punishments this past year, including disruption, failure to follow instructions, destruction of property, and torturing the class hedgehog, all the while directing Steele for the hour and a half drive; one excruciatingly endless monologue.

Chandni competently navigated Steele to the fairgrounds, and they agreed to check in with each other later in the afternoon at the Cleveland Cyclone, Sidd's favorite ride.

Where to begin the search for Jacob? Begin the begin, as Micheal Stipe sang.

At the ticket counter Steele asked where he could find Jacob.

The pimply teenage girl shrugged. "Who?"

"Nevermind."

Blinking lights bombarded Steele's senses, and hunger pangs reminded him nearly a day passed since his last meal. Browsing the county fair's culinary cornucopia he selected Twice Fried Peanut Butter and Jelly Sticks, after Deep Fried Bologna and Butter Batons.

Satiated with a gut full of grease Steele refocused on his task, aware that noon fast approached. "Hey, how can I find Jacob Steele?" He asked a ride operator with symmetrical scars from the far corners of his eyes to the bottom of his earlobes.

The man visibly winced at the name. "Don't know 'im. You wanna ride? No line yet."

"Jacob Steele, he's an owner of the company? It's an urgent private matter. Family matter."

Cryer never heard Jake talk of no family. Best he knew Jake never married, rarely ever found a woman for the night, didn't have any sisters, brothers, or parents. "Nope, don't know who you talkin' about."

Steele received the same reaction from each worker he talked with: a cringe or grimace, followed by denial. Yet every ride and game displayed the company's name. Getting nowhere, Steele snacked on Sausage and Maple Syrup Fritters to consider another approach. If Rosa were here, she'd think of some way to find him. What would Rosa do?

***

News travelled to Jake that a tall, thin guy with blonde curly hair asked nearly every jointee and showman for him. The guy wouldn't say more than he wanted to talk about an urgent family matter, though he looked like a government type.

Ranger hadn't called yet from Utah, even though he'd been gone three days. The codger usually kept a line open to Jake nearly every day, and now some pesky punk's tryin' to find him about some family matter. Family didn't matter to him.

Figurin' he'd have some fun with the guy, he sent word to make the guy find the key to the midway and bring it to the Cleveland Cyclone at four. At least he'd be able to check out the imbecile. Fool, he thought; hope he brought his ATM card, the gaffs will suck his account like an eleven-year-old on a helium balloon teat.

***

After a round of Deep Fried Refried Bean Rods, Steele's body sagged from oversaturation and little exertion, unsettled with collywobbles. How many times could beans be fried anyhow? He plopped on a bench in broad view of the midway games for his stomach to accommodate the day's abuses.

Last time he plopped on a public bench Spring Break had ended and classes resumed on campus. He watched students stroll from building to building. The Spring tabling tournament kicked off that week too, as clubs recruited others to their causes in the quad. Some displayed artifacts. Others erected flashy propaganda posters. The more financially flush clubs offered incentives (or bribes, if one agreed with the acerbic editorials of the student newspaper).

Steele merged the midway and collegiate tabling, wondering if midway gamesmanship might make effective recruitment hooks for student clubs. Sign this petition to curb investment in Israel, win a goldfish. Support labor rights in Guatemala, take home an oversized plush dolphin. Squirt water in the clown's mouth to fight desertification in Nigeria. Save the ozone layer by popping three balloons with two darts.

He could meld midway games for zealous athletic fanatics into a new genre of competitive sport. A pentathlon of intercollegiate athletic games with loose rope ladders, mallet pounding, rigged basketball, milk bottle softball pitching, and ring tossing pitting players' dexterity, patience, and strength.

To really build hysteria in crowds, he'd figure out how to make it a contact sport—play them simultaneously in mud with four offensive players and three defensive players, perhaps. Daydreaming about competitive intramural midway sports triggered an idea flash.

He grabbed footballs inflated like boulders from a football-shaped man, trusting his arm to miss mightily. And did. Repeat, this time peeling twice the money for five throws. Missed each one. Again, the gruff-voiced gamester tempted him. Certainly, Steele agreed; insisting on information rather than five more throws.

"Yeah, Jake's here. Bring the key to the midway to the Cleveland Cyclone at four." The boisterous, mullet-wearing carny baited Steele.

Skeptical, and desperate to take any lead, Steele followed the crumb. "Where do I get the key to the midway? What does it look like?" Steele fingered the cabin key around his neck.

"Check with the other games, they'll help ya. Start with the coin toss over there," and thumb-pointed three booths down.

"One more thing," Steele added another note from his wallet, "what's he look like?"

"Tall and thin. Always wearin' a tight red shirt and overalls. And, he's got a voice, like…well, like a cartoon. Like a wimperin' puppy under my boot—and I weigh in at 280 before breakfast. Go try the dime toss, tell him Big Gary sent ya."

The dime toss kid, not yet able to grow more than a shadow above his lip, clued Steele to collect prizes from six games—he'd already walked away with a toy football. Bring the six to the Cleveland Coaster at four. One prize must be the six-foot purple dinosaur, hanging above most the games. "But that's only for you to know, since Big Gary sent ya. Go to the Tubs of Fun ball bounce after here."

"Big Gary? Sure," the pony-tailed brute shared a sly wink with Steele, "you just gotta get two balls into the bin, like this." The carny tossed the heavier softballs with a high arc, giving them an imperceptible backspin to minimize the hidden spring's reaction and handed Steele the lighter, cork-filled balls.

Pleased with his strategic cleverness Steele gladly tossed rings on bottles, bounced balls off oblong rims, shot out paper stars with BBs, and aimed water streams at clowns' gaping mouths— 'winning' chimerical souvenirs manufactured by children toiling across the globe for a pittance. Steele blithely succumbed to the gaudy entrapments, reluctantly dwindling down his bank balance. By his third trip to the ATM the price of this elusive midway key climbed to a week's salary.

Burdened by gimcracks and gewgaws, baubles and beads, trifles and trinkets, Steele penetrated a gasping crowd at the Cleveland Cyclone. The catawampus monstrosity seemed designed to decapitate steer by centrifugal force rather than for the fleeting amusement of overindulged, pouting rapscallions. Steele immediately recognized the boy who scaled the apparatus. Sidd.

Height at his advantage, Steele scanned the congregated mass for Chandni. He shoved forward, politely excusing himself and his menagerie as the crowd thickened closer to the cantilever contraption.

"Mr. Steele," Chandni hugged him instinctively, "Sidd's up there. One second we were all in line, the next he'd already climbed part way up," her panic-drenched voice teetered on tears. She pointed up with one hand, squeezing her other brother's hand so tightly his fingertips darkened.

Steele yelled to the carny, "You call 911?"

"Yup," Steele recognized him from earlier in the day, one of the half dozen or so who brushed him off while he asked around for Jacob, "firemen are at the gate now."

A tall, lean man with sun-caramelized skin in a red shirt and blue overalls mounted the ride's entrance platform. Through a blow horn his cartoon rodent voice calmly and assuredly persuaded the crowd to part as the fire engine approached.

From the platform Jake tagged the sap burdened with midway garbage at the front of the mass, sticking out like an albino alligator.

Jake immediately, unquestionably knew.

As if seeing himself at age twenty-seven.

As if seeing his father.

The boy born from Ka.

Police statements given, Rajesh and Madhup arrived to claim their miscreant and his siblings in the carnival's office trailer. In his anger at Steele's irresponsible chaperoning he demanded Steele return their minivan immediately. Steele refused, his business unfinished.

Rajesh and Steele bickered over degrees of irresponsibility—a parent sending his children with a stranger to a county fair while entrusting a teenager to supervise her brothers? Or a man with a game-playing compulsion ignoring minors entrusted to his care? Jake hovered nearby, occasionally piping orders at workers, finally stepping in to settle the scene.

The power of cash, a level headed wife, all Steele's useless bounty, and ample vouchers for concession food thrown in by the company convinced Rajesh to back down. The family merged into the masses.

A cloud laden with anticipation and disbelief ensconced Jake and Steele. Once alone the two men hesitated; each hoping the other might speak first.

"What the hell do you want?" Jake squealed, betraying no emotion.

"You are Jacob Steele, your father is Levi Steele, correct?"

Jake nodded, emitting a muffled noise between a birdsong and a police siren.

"I'm Thurgood Levi Steele."

"Yeah. What the hell do you want?"

Not much for small talk, Steele thought. "Well, I brought news. Bad news."

"Did the old man die?"

Steele nodded.

"Good riddance. Never liked 'im much." Jake moved some folders on the desk, more from inability to remain still than any attempt at organization, Steele surmised. He knocked an empty, stained coffee mug with a glowing Ferris wheel on Steele's foot, shrugging one shoulder as a half-hearted apology.

With decades to formulate questions, training in historical investigation methodologies, and dozens of family rumors to probe Steele found himself unable to assemble a coherent question. He vacantly blurted, "There's a will. You need to be at the attorney's office for the reading, this Friday." As Steele leaned forward to retrieve the mug the distinct, oblong key flumped from his shirt with a sharp clink on the ceramic.

Jake flinched at sight of the key.

"Where'd that key come from?"

Instinctively Steele grabbed the necklace. "A friend found it in the woods."

"In a cabin?"

A nod.

"Ever use it? To open the door?" Jake asked.

"What door?"

"Damn, ya don't know 'bout the cabin door? That's a pisser. What did the old man say 'bout me?"

"Not much. Talked about your talents with machines and cars. He seemed irked by your total disinterest with books, with family history. With any history. He said you just left one day, not long after Marika left, when I was only an infant."

"Did he 'splain that he screwed us over twice? Family used ta own half that town, practic'ly. First, he stopped farmin'. We coulda been pumpin' apples to Japan, makin' better cheddar than the Brits. He cut those off, closed it all down. Rather sit and read books than be outside, damn lazy ass.

"Then he sold the land, and ev'n gave some away free. That ain't no way to honor family history, the hard work of ancestors. Damn guy was a hypocrite. Loved his family stories, but wouldn' lift a goddamn finger to do what they did for a livin'.

"I couldn't sit 'round and do nothin' all day. Still can't. Need to be workin' with my hands, massagin' machines, fixin' things to make kids happy. Apples make kids happy. So do rides and games. And these fairs," Jake gestured broadly as if an opera singer closing a climatic aria, "make me a ton of money. I don't want even one goddamn cent from him. I buried him decades ago."

"Just like you buried me." Steele shocked himself with the raw statement. His emotional volcano erupted. Those tortuous decades of anguish flooded Steele's being. Flashes of curling on his bed, shaking with anger at being discarded. The plans of suicide, abandoned only for Papa's love. Suffering years from lack of self-worth, stifled self-respect, confidence drowned in the river of rejection by Jacob and Marika. His steel gaze masked his wrenching inner turmoil.

Jacob peered at Steele like he'd been pierced with an arrow near his heart. Like a wounded animal, Jake fled out the trailer door. He'd always run.

Steele lunged after him, reaching for Jacob's shoulder but missing.

They didn't get far.

Just three strides out Eddie Tang turned a corner, nearly colliding with Jake.

Eddie grabbed Jake's arm, "Jake. There's news from Southwest Smiles. Ranger's dead."

Eddie's news stopped Jake, a real puncture in his heart. "No," he shook his head, "no, no fuckin' way."

Eddie remained there, other crew supervisors trickling around, forming a circle with Eddie, Steele, and Jake in the middle.

Steele wondered who Ranger is, or was, and glanced at the four foot letters on the trailer's side, *Ranger Rides and Steele Shows, Inc.: Making Kids of All Ages Smile.*

"He just dropped walkin' down the midway," Eddie added.

"Shoulda been near the rides." Jake groped for humor. No one smiled. He noticed the ride jocks gatherin' round, ordered them back to work. "There's thousands of fuckin' people payin' for a goddamn good time. Make it happen!"

Eddie, Jake, and Steele retreated to the office trailer, sitting in Ranger's small living area at the rear. Eddie withdrew a small bag and rolling papers from his pocket, dropping them on the tiny table. Steele waved it off. Eddie rolled one, ceremoniously handing it to Jake. Jake held it, not lighting it.

Eddie looked between the two lanky, slim men noting the uncanny resemblance. Wagging a finger between them he asked the obvious, "You two related?"

No reaction from Jake.

Steele nodded.

"Brothers?" Eddie guessed.

No response from Jake or Steele.

"You his son?" He guessed again, directly at Steele.

"Let him tell you." Steele pointed to Jake with a slight head twist.

Jake ignored Eddie's question, rolling the unlit joint between his fingers mindlessly. "My father's dead," he announced.

"What kinda work you do?" Jake asked Steele, unexpectedly.

"I'm a professor. A history professor in New York City."

"Well, just like the old man, then, eh? Good for you. At least you gettin' paid to read all them books. You ever look at land records for the family?"

Steele silently shook his head, no.

"You go do that. I'm gonna take care of Ranger, 'cause he took care of me. A helluva lot more than Levi ever cared."

Steele doubted that, remembering when Papa most directly spoke about Jacob just last summer. "*He left, but he is still one of us by birthright. That can never be erase*d." Papa's eyes paused on the single framed photo of Jacob, around eleven years old, with him in the woods. In front of a cabin, Steele suddenly recalled. He rebuked Jake, "You're wrong. He cared. At the deepest part of his soul, he cared. He never healed from your disappearance."

"Whatever," Jake dismissed Steele's proclamation waving his hand with the unlit joint. "Leave the details. I'm not sayin' I'll be there; not sayin' I won't, neither." He tossed the joint to Eddie, stood, unfurled his lean limbs.

Jake strode out the dim trailer into the brilliant raucous harmony of grunting machines, teenage screams, and smiles everywhere. Home.

SEALED
2000 Nineteen

Thankfully, Rosa answered the phone. Steele had no patience this morning to navigate either of his newly acquired half-sisters or Marika, and figured Carlos would just hang up. He appreciated that the only phone in the house, a corded and wall-mounted relic, could still be hung up.

"Did you find him?" she asked in a hushed tone, not wanting to wake anyone.

"Yes, thanks to the key to the midway and a rambunctious, troublesome boy."

"What boy? And the key Drew gave you?" She sounded confused.

"Sorry, never mind the boy. Or the key. Long story. But yes, I found Jacob."

"So, will he come Friday?"

"I don't know. Someone else he knew, a guy called Ranger, died yesterday somewhere out west. He said he's going to take care of Ranger."

"As in Ranger Rides and Steele Shows?"

"I think so," pre-boarding announcements for Steele's flight injected a pause, "anyway, are you set to fly?"

"We have our tickets. It's been wonderful seeing them all again. But...," she stopped.

"But?" He wondered aloud.

"But, well, Mama keeps that old letter nearby. The one with your name across it. She touches it, loses the conversation thread for a moment when she does. You never opened it, right?"

"Um-hmm, right," the counter attendant announced general boarding, interrupting them again. "I've got to board now, when do you get in?"

Steele took the arrival details, promised to meet them on Thursday.

PUN FOR ONE
2000 Twenty

Steele drove to Mr. D's for a quick slice and a soda before heading to the octagon-shaped library, its poodle-skirt porch beckoning for lemonade-infused humid afternoons. Time gliding past him, Steele wasted no time lazily lollygagging with loquacious locals. A search for land parcels in the family name generated results on old paper maps, draining time. The clerk keyed the surnames Stegenga and Halstead with similarly ambiguous results. He wished he could search by zooming on a map, but the town's website lacked the sophistication of the university.

He ventured south to Poughkeepsie using Route 9 passing estates of Ogden Mills and Vanderbilt, the Roosevelt Presidential Library, the Culinary Institute of America, and Marist College; by osmosis seeping in the vast historical eras and tremendous wealth represented by each campus. From the height of industry and global power, to the pinnacle of knowledge and culinary genius, history oozed on every acre. Plenty for a lifetime of research, he reflected, hoping his employment might be salvageable with desperate groveling to the provost.

Inside the nondescript county government building, in a plain room, behind a normal desk Steele enlisted support from a pudgy lady in a tight fitting purple dress with identical lilac lipstick who introduced herself as Violet—providing the finest bipedal eggplant impersonation Steele ever witnessed. After understanding what he sought she disappeared behind a wall, to reappear with several binders. "We're building a new computerized system, because the last one stopped working. I need a *crash* course to learn it." She paused with an odd grin. "What parcels are we looking for again?"

He explained.

"And what's the at*trac*tion?" She emphasized the middle syllable, clueing Steele to her game.

"*Real* funny," he retorted, playing along to garner her in partnership, unlike most of his recent plans.

"Okay, the land around the school is in the name of the AFPF Trust," she offered.

"Does it list an address for the trust?"

"In*deed*. A legal office in Kingston," she smirked in the peculiarly pleased manner of self-aggrandized punners.

Were he the kind to roll his eyes, this would be the time. Steele jotted down the familiar address in the Roundout neighborhood and pushed forward, "Do any other parcels belong to AFPF Trust?"

"I'll be right back, that's in the *ABC*—the *A*lphabetical *B*inder, *see*?" the punning human aubergine promised.

Steele inspected the lonely poster when she disappeared around the corner, stating recent changes in ad valorem assessment procedures. He pitied the person who wrote such droll content.

She returned, already leafing through the document. "Yes, four other parcels. All in Rhinebeck and Red Hook. All undeveloped land, or zoned for agriculture. Hope that attorney is *trust*worthy," she reported. Steele forced a painful grin.

"Can you copy this list for me?"

She pointed to a sign, listing the price per copy as a dime per page. "That makes *sense*, rather than writing it by hand," he agreed just to escape the pitiful purple person's painstakingly pointless puns.

REFRESHING
2000 Twenty-One

Curiosity niggled Steele since that memory flash about the cabin with Jacob. Back in Papa's house, Steele retrieved the photo of Jacob and Papa from among the frames on display in the living room. Jacob's features at that age struck Steele as uncannily familiar. He hunted photos of himself at age eleven from his boyhood room-cum-R.E.M shrine.

Shifting his mindset from object of the images to a professional investigator examining photographic artifacts for evidence, similarities rose like the pop-up artwork of children's books. Levi, Jacob, and Thurgood shared angular noses, deep set eyes and blond curly hair. The body structures of the two boys replicated each other, as if struck from the same mold. Their lips curled in similar forced grins, and comparable hairlines rounded their faces. Uncanny how these expressions of genetic traits spanned the generations of the family, Steele noted.

Papa and Jacob stood frozen in time, a cabin's corner of freshly cut logs behind them on the right side of the frame. Wood chips and tools lay scattered in the left side of the frame on the ground, with a stovepipe visible a short distance behind them.

The cabin. The key. The same attorney Papa used for his will, also the registered agent representing the land trust for former

Steele/Stagenga/Halstead holdings.

Rosa's call jarred his concentration. She reconfirmed logistics and assured him all was well, but melancholy and resignation tinged her voice.

Steele dialed Drew on his cell phone. Not dialed, really; he hadn't used a rotary phone since Papa surrendered to technology's advancement in 1989 with a cordless push button phone. One cannot dial on a cell phone. One simply calls.

The friends rendezvoused at the Rhinecliff Hotel once more, a fast-talking, heavily-accented muscular man serving the rounds who called himself Austin. Enthralled by the structure, its history, and its context in the area, rumors of Steele's expertise circulated to him before Steele's arrival. Struggling to suppress his professor's urges to share his knowledge with the bartender, Steele focused on Drew, promising a lecture later. Drew barely met Steele's eyes.

"No more about *That Night*, Steele. God, when is enough enough for you?" Exasperation saturated Drew's tone.

"I'm sorry, Drew. A lot happened to us *That Night*. *That Night* changed our lives, forced me to confront death and dying for the first time. I've finally realized my life is sculpted by loss."

"You mean Chris?" he said, matter-of-factly.

Shivers crawled down Steele's back. Did Drew just utter their lost friend's name, so seldom had he uttered the name since his disappearance? Steele blinked at Drew in disbelief.

"Get over it, Steele. Chris died *That Night*. He's gone. Saying his name honors his life. Keeps his memory alive." Drew drained his first beer of the night, a light ale.

"Not just Chris." Speaking his name granted Steele an immediate ameliorative release. "Since birth, I've been abandoned. Intentionally, or not. This past week I've realized the losses have enriched my experiences, defined my journey in this world. Focusing on the emptiness distracted me from embracing the strengths I've developed." Over the span of two more rounds—an Irish red, then a deep chocolaty stout; both new additions to the bar's staid selections—Steele detailed the nearly sabotaged pursuit of Marika, her second rejection of him, and her ultimate agreement to travel for the reading on Friday.

Steele boasted how he outsmarted the carnies to ultimately meet Jacob face to face. Carefully and intentionally Steele circled back to the key Drew resurrected from the debris *That Night*, picking up that Jacob asked about using the key in the cabin.

"That girlfriend of yours didn't tell you?" Drew asked, doubtful.

"Tell me what?"

Plain and simple Drew stated, "The key opens a cellar door in that cabin. I opened it *That Night.*"

Why hadn't Drew told him this before? Steele opened his mouth to ask as the bartender interrupted. "Another round, guys?" The bartender seemed on the verge of gushing questions, his wide eyes familiar to Steele from his most engaged students.

"An Irish Red for him, water for me," Steele ordered.

"There's nothing there." Drew answered definitively before Steele could ask. "Just darkness. No more."

The comfortable stillness of long friendship visited the pair as Drew sipped his beer. The bartender hovered nearby.

"Steele, life is lived forward, not in reverse," Drew advised. "Get over it."

The future is built on the past, Steele thought on his way to the restroom. Reentering the bar after the reprieve, animated chatter between the bartender and Drew brightened the mood. Passing by the pair to the jukebox Steele overheard Drew emphasize, "some people say they see a horse standing near the tracks down there," thumbing towards the river. The bartender looked enchanted by that old ghost story, Steele thought.

To Steele's amazement the jukebox's options had been updated with some of last year's alternative music hits including Santana and Rob Thomas with *Smooth*, the Red Hot Chili Peppers' *Scar Tissue*, and Lenny Kravitz's *Fly Away*. Drew and Ross burst into laughter, so Steele selected *Shiny Happy People*, one of R.E.M.'s bounciest and upbeat recordings; paid the tab and left the flirting men.

A PIZZA MOMENT
2000 Twenty-Two

Rosa melted into Steele's embrace at the airport. Marika offered a tentative handshake.

"I have less than thirty-six hours then I'm back in the dragon's lair. Gossip of my daughter marrying the son I abandoned at birth kicked the local media into a frenzy. But it doubled my name recognition overnight," Marika declared. "None of that matters here. I came to clear my conscience, to state my truth, damn the consequences."

Steele pointed the car south using the Taconic Parkway, with unsurpassed vistas of the Catskills and Taconic Mountains, its narrow lanes deemed too tight for commercial vehicles. Marika soaked in the undulating beauty of this region. Gone too long, she thought.

Determined to squeeze all the juice from this visit, Marika directed Steele down the dirt road towards the river when they arrived in Red Hook. The road no longer navigable by car, they walked, Marika nostalgic and glad to be outdoors on a nearly perfect early summer afternoon. The breeze, trees, and bird calls triggered Marika's glimpses of the days before she left; momentarily eradicating the decades since she and Jake coupled there.

"In high school and middle school, my friends and I rode

bikes here, came fishing, partied occasionally," Steele offered to start a conversation. Freshly scattered beer cans, soda bottles, and food wrappers littered the space between the railroad tracks and the water, witness to the current generation of partiers.

"Jake drove me here in his LeMans, he loved that old car...," Marika drifted off, "I'd dream of my hippie utopia out west; he'd rage at his father, bristling to leave school and make money. The signs were so obvious that we were on entirely different tracks. We'd smoke pot, get drunk, have sex down here—the chemicals and the carnal pleasure connected us, nothing deeper."

"We dropped acid too here. Stupid teenagers," Marika reminisced. As if a switch clicked, she turned to Steele, "Is Mr. D's still around? I'd love a good slice. Can't find quality pizza in Deming." She reversed and charged up the trail, never glancing back to the river.

"Just like I remember," Marika savored the memory (and the sauce), narrating stories of after-hours exploits with Jake in the parking lot, out of view of the road. Gesturing east and west, north and south she sketched monstrous winter storms and cherished girlhood crushes; a sprained ankle and her first lost tooth tripping on the sidewalk a block away. Details flooded back, long forgotten until the visual triggers and an eager audience in Steele and Rosa.

"There's a cabin not too far away. Not too deep in the woods. Do you know it? I think it belongs to your family," Marika directed at Steele.

Steele replied carefully, "I know of a cabin—rather, the remains of a cabin—not too far from here. Whether it's the same one, who knows?" He lightly tapped the key around his neck.

"Take me there," she demanded with a persuasive smile.

REMAINING OODLES
2000 Twenty-Three

Heading west towards the river, Steele angled towards one of the parcels Violet listed as under the ownership of the AFPF Trust, adjacent to an old growth preservation park.

Steele noticed Marika growing increasingly uneasy within the short ten-minute drive, while he grasped the key around his neck every half minute as if it might vanish.

With the car parked halfway in a culvert, Steele scavenged a flashlight from the glove compartment despite dusk's distant onset.

"Got any bug spray?" Rosa requested.

"Nope, sorry," Steele wished he would have remembered some. "Okay, I hope this is the way. It's been many, many years and there's a lot of growth this season."

Thick underbrush, briars, and uncertain direction blended into slow progress. Steele scanned for familiar signs—the fallen tree at the edge of the swamp, the granite outcropping beside the seasonal stream—but none appeared.

He led them up a small knoll where they paused to survey the surroundings.

Steele scanned the area, hoping to find a clue. Nothing. They rested, he pondered the next step.

"Well, ain't that just the shit," the harsh voice blurted a too familiar phrase, "if it ain't Mr. Steele and…Mary, no…."

"Marika," Marika helped him, "and you are?"

"Darryl, Darryl Cooper. I used to hang out with Jake a bit in high school. Never really outside school so much. Didn't he and you date?"

"Darryl," Steele interrupted, "what are you doing out here?"

"Might ask you the same. I ain't caught you out since the night you was out near Fiddler's Bridge. Just doin' my job. Watchin' over this land."

One of the other parcels for the AFPF Trust abutted Fiddler's Bridge, according to the purple punner in Poughkeepsie. "Who do you work for, Darryl?"

"I ain't allowed to say. But seein' as you all look lost, I can help you out. Gotta git you out anyhow. Where'd you get in from?"

"We're looking for a cabin, or the remains of a cabin, somewhere near here. You know about it?" Marika smiled charmingly.

"Yeah, I s'pose it ain't gonna hurt no one. You drove in from Pernhally Road, right? I seen a car over there on the side, half-cocked parking."

Steele nodded sheepishly.

"You all passed it a ways back. Not much left these days, just an old barrel stove half rusted to nuthin'. Kids' been back kickin' that apart for years. Come on, that's the way to your car."

Darryl hobbled back the path they came from, a stump sized brace around one ankle, a baseball bat serving as a cane. They fell in line behind him. Marika, Steele, then Rosa at the rear.

Darryl occasionally grimaced and mumbled when stepping on the braced leg. He shouted over his shoulder, Steele able to catch a snippet, "Damn doc said not to put much weight on my ankle, how the hell am I s'possed to do that?"

The sun inched closer to the horizon, Steele guessing about an hour left before sundown when they arrived at the cabin. Or, what Darryl confirmed as the place where a cabin used to be.

"Ain't this just the shit. Someone's done taken the stove. What the hell they gonna do with a rusted heap of metal?"

"You sure this is the place?" Steele questioned.

"Yup. One way to tell," Darryl used the bat to prod the ground, limping around the site.

Thick leaf fall muffled the thuds. He continued.

"Should be right about here," he dropped the bat again, with a flat hollow din bellowing up. "Yup. Guy that built it put a cellar out here. Don't know why, don't make no sense to me."

Steele clutched the key. Began clearing leaves. Kicked them aside at first. Dropped to his knees, dug with bare hands.

"Whatcha doin'? Ain't nothin' in there. We gotta go." Darryl demanded. Steele ignored him.

Marika stood frozen beside Rosa. She clasped Rosa's hand, Rosa holding tight. Tears welled in Marika's eyes. Vaulted tears, the crypt now pried open on this spot. Marika hugged Rosa, nearly collapsing into her for support. No words could capture the anguish roiling in Marika at the injustice, the humiliation, the violation. So many years ago, yet so vivid. Rosa guided Marika to a small lump of moss-covered logs, the last vestige of the cabin's wall. Marika fully collapsed into Rosa, convulsing in sobbing waves. Rosa scrambled to support her mother's full weight, fretfully asked, "Mama, qué pasa?" The two women clung to each other. Marika gestured off Rosa's question.

Darryl, speechless for once, his mouth open, gaping.

Oblivious to Marika's breakdown, Steele scraped away debris until the keyhole emerged.

He inserted the key. Partially.

"It's clogged with dirt. Rosa do you have a..., " he turned, found her fully holding Marika up. "What's going on? Is she okay? Is she hurt?"

Marika's sobs began to subside. "Not hurt," she waved, wiping away tears. "Too much, all at once," she sniffled, then dug out a tissue to clear her nose.

"I'll take care of her. What do you need?"

Steele surrendered concerns about Marika to Rosa's care, for the moment. "A pin, water, something to clear this keyhole."

He flicked dirt out with a pocketknife Darryl produced, cleared it enough for the key to completely enter.

Turned the key.

Felt a pop, the door slightly bounced.

Steele heaved, rotated the substantial door on a creaking hinge, thudding it open, upsetting leaves in small whirlwinds.

He shined the powerful flashlight beam inside.

Several grimy Cheezey Oodles bags lay scattered on dank soil below, alongside mold-ridden remains curled in a fetal position, a bud that never blossomed, beside an overturned urn spilling an ash floe. A rank stench emanated out, so powerfully putrid it knocked Steele backward, as if he inhaled death's final exhale.

MIDWAY REMAINS
2000 Twenty-Four

"I'm as next of kin as he's got," Jake insisted to the morgue's clerk, a young tanned woman in a tight, brightly flowered shirt and scarlet lipstick, handing his Florida license to her.

"You're from Gibsonton? I'm from Brandon. We're neighbors, yeah? What a coincidence!" She shuffled off to copy his ID so he could claim the body, returning with a clipboard and form.

"Go in there," she pointed to the gray door.

Jake entered the space, a sterile room with no noise, only one body. Ranger. The young bloom joined him.

"You know him?"

Jake nodded. "See that scar next to his ear? Told me he was takin' apart a wood coaster when he was fifteen, a board smacked him upside his head, screw scraped him. Lost some hearing in that ear from it."

"Complete the form. Find me there." She pointed at the desk. "Take your time."

Not sure why, he spoke out loud after she left. Felt like the right thing to do. "Ranger, you ol' shit. What the hell I'm gonna do without ya? You're the closest I got to fam'ly." He wiped his mouth with his palm. Remember that boy, he'd been a baby when I joined up with ya? He found me, we was in Taylor

County and he come along. Told me my old man kicked it. Wants me to go to New York for the will readin'," Jake stopped, half hoping Ranger might pop up, or grin and tell him it's all a joke. Ranger remained dead. "But you was needin' me. So, I'm here. We been workin' together what, twenty-six years, thereabouts? I lived with Levi eighteen years. He raised me good, I guess; never went hungry and he never hit me. But when he done give all the land away, he gave away my future. I ain't never gonna forgive that, Ranger, never. Let 'im roll in his grave." The chill of the sterile room struck Jake.

"The boy looks like me. Stands like me, face like mine. Spittin' image. He's a history professor in the city. Damn smart kid. Guess Levi didn't screw him up."

The desk blossom poked her head in the door. "Funeral home's here. Bury, or cremate?"

"Cremate."

"Okay, got it. I'll tell them." She left the room again.

"Damn, Ranger. I ain't sure I want to go. Gonna be a hell of a long time away from the show. Now that you're gone, I ain't got no one."

Ranger's words seeped through Jake's memory from one of the winter breaks when they'd visited a cemetery near Ruskin for Ranger's buried relatives, where one of the brothers of the escaped Alcatraz prisoners was also buried. *Everythin' I ever got I got from family. They all died off on me. I miss 'em, even the ones done piss me off ev'ry day. Still regret what I never said to them out loud.*

The budding girl returned. "Excuse me, sir? They're outside waiting. Are you ready?"

"Yeah, I'm ready. How long does it take to burn 'im?"

"Five days, sir. The whole process. Start to finish. Preparation first day. Cremation next day. Waiting period after. Required by law." She tapped the clipboard. "Sign the forms."

WALKING ENTOMBED
2000 Twenty-Five

That blasted cell phone proved worthwhile when Steele called 9-1-1, he reasoned, finally justifying toting it everywhere—but how often does one discover the decomposed body of a friend lost more than a decade earlier in a nearly forgotten cabin's hidden cellar?

A reporter from the Poughkeepsie Journal arrived minutes after the police, tipped off by the emergency services scanner, kicking off another round of investigations into Chris's cold case disappearance. After leaving the cabin and dropping Marika at the Beekman Arms Inn, he called Drew to meet at the Rhinecliff Hotel. Marika insisted that Rosa go with Steele.

Opposite Steele, Drew nestled beside Rosa in the graffiti-laden booth, obvious irritation across his face.

"Sorry, Drew. This couldn't wait. We found Chris's body."

Drew stared at the table, seemingly unmoved at the news. "At the burned old cabin?"

Steele peered quizzically at Drew, Drew's question sounded as if Steele just discovered bees make honey. "But, how…? "

Drew inhaled deeply, hands starting to tremble so slightly.

"There's a dream that's haunted me ever since *That Night*. Used to come a lot, but less frequent now. It was happening when you called me tonight. In the dream, the key floats overhead. I'm drowning under soil, in blackness. It's hard to describe." Drew stopped to draw breath again, clearly becoming jittery. "I sense Chris when I wake up from that dream. It's been a hunch of mine for a long while, that he's been down there. I've never been able to bring myself to go and see—all these years with the key, and I've never gone." Drew paused, voice cracking from suppressed emotions now bubbling like carbonation in beer. "Sorry, I'm not explaining it well." He breathed deeply, intently, remorsefully, Steele thought.

Drew cleared his throat, failing to choke down his voice's shakiness. "*That Night* I opened the door with the key when rummaging the old cabin. Left it slightly open. I remember clearly. My hunch about Chris is that he went in there to hide, to figure out what to do after shooting his father. If I hadn't taken the key, maybe he'd still be alive." Tears gathered in the corners of Drew's eyes, like morning dew dripping down composting leaves with the first ray of sunlight. He smeared them with the back of his freckled hand.

Rosa grasped Drew's forearm beside her. "It's not your fault. That boy killed his own father. If the cops found him, he'd be in jail. His life changed forever when he pulled the trigger."

"Drew, you told me to live my life forward, not in reverse. Just last night, right here," Steele jammed the tacky table top with his finger.

Drew sprang from the booth nearly dumping the table in his friend's lap, shouting "Dammit, Steele. I've carried his death on my shoulders more than half my LIFE, hoping that he might have LIVED, somehow. Now you want me to just forget it, after you tell me you found his body? That's bullshit." Drew stepped closer to Steele. "I've tried for YEARS to ignore it. Did okay for a while, too. Since you've been back after your Papa died and resurrected all this, it's haunted me again. It's dragging me down. I can't focus on anything else."

Steele stood to be at eye level with Drew. "Drew, please—" he pleaded with his friend, only to be cut off.

"Chris is not coming back, Steele. He'll never have a career, an education, children, or a chance at love. If I hadn't left that door ajar maybe, someday he'd have a chance." Visibly quivering, Drew's face reddened.

Steele moved closer to his friend's side. "It's not your fault, Drew. *HE* stole the gun and shot his father. *HE* ran away. You had no way of knowing any of that was happening. Come on, sit down," Steele pointed to Rosa's bench, "none of us knew what *That Night* would bring."

Steele returned to the worn bench, Drew collapsing beside him. In a hushed, defeated voice he leaned into Steele, whispers that left Rosa out of the exchange. "*That Night* I was drugged— twice. Then raped by our English teacher. Then Chris disappeared. And you—your Papa grounded you for a couple months—you got off easy. I've been paying the price since then. And I'm done, Steele. Done. I'm making changes, starting now." Dropping to near silence by the end, he squeezed Steele's forearm.

Drew hugged Rosa, rounded the bar to kiss Austin, and stepped out the bar's door, turning left towards the river.

GREEN TUNES
2000 Twenty-Six

Finally alone with Rosa, Steele collapsed from exhaustion. With the pace of events Steele sidelined the grieving process for Papa, only just beginning to fully accept his passing. The meeting with the attorney—and Marika—and Jacob, if he comes—now half a day away. The sluice box of the last two weeks yielded one nugget thus far, wrapped around him in the darkest hour of the night. Rosa's calm, subtle assurances lulled him to sleep.

Until the doorbell chimed and pounding thundered the door. Flashes of That Night rattled Steele.

Steele jumped. Disoriented and woken from his first deep rest in days, he opened the door with Rosa shadowing him, an unseasonable chilly air filtering in, dawn barely bubbling over the horizon.

Drew drowned. Apparent suicide, Officer Van der Waals reported. Steele heard nothing else after that.

He stumbled backward, grabbing the wall and Rosa for support. Not now. No. This would be a cruel nightmare. He'd wake up beside Rosa, rekindle the intimacy of the night. He crumbled on the step, numb. Too much loss, too much upheaval. Steele's nascent stability became engulfed in a tornado, losing complete sense of up and down, fragments of reality impaling him. Drew's death nudged Steele to a precipice.

Rosa ushered him to the bedroom, returning to the police for her statement. She summed the trauma Steele endured recently. Of the critical meeting later that day. Rosa assured the officer Steele would provide a statement, implored her to return later. Reluctantly she agreed.

Rosa found him in shock, unable to rest again. Could he handle her news about her cycle delaying? Not likely. Not now. Another time, she postponed that conversation.

"Did that just happen?" he asked her. "Did the cop say Drew died?"

Rosa held his hand, sitting on the bed's edge. "I don't know what to say. You've suffered more than anyone should in a lifetime, just in the last few weeks."

"Yesterday, with Marika at Mr. D's, I felt as if I began rebuilding my life. I finally relaxed and enjoyed the moment, the pizza, her stories of a lifetime ago.

"There's been no time for us to even talk about how she's dealing with our relationship. Or how you two are getting along. I haven't talked with you about Jacob either. If he doesn't show up, there may be no future. My job likely ended by administrative termination, did I mention that?"

Rosa massaged his arm, listening.

"And Chris…," Steele dropped. And remained silent, his heart rendered raw. He shut his eyes, not sleeping, unable to move, unable to think. Images of the lost visited him. Of Papa nestled with a book. Of Chris lounging beside the pool, savoring his synth-pop music. Of Drew bumbling through a story as a teen; of his portly, beard-fringed face tonight.

Steele succumbed to the pain, overwhelmed under the torturous depths of sorrow. Each boulder of damage, the cumulative losses a crushing, mountainous weight.

A solo fiddler's spirit fused with Steele. Accompanied him in shock and pain. As the searing torment raged through Steele's reality, the fiddler consoled him with lingering empathetic notes. The tuneful vibrations touched Steele beneath his cairn, a tingle of light in the cellar of darkness. The fiddler's intonations guided Steele through the dense maze of desperation, illuminating the cracks to the surface with a verdant hue. The fiddler's song intensified as Steele toed a tentative step into the light.

Rosa busied herself with cleaning and organizing—the irony of stereotypical activities not lost on her—yet from immediate satisfaction of her efforts. She assured herself that Steele would be beside her if not crumpled in a grieving cocoon, resisting her urges to lay beside him.

As noon approached she inched open the door where Steele rested, two hours before his lawyer's appointment. The sheets and his body reeked of expelled illness; a sweat-stained ring encircled him despite the refreshing Chamber of Commerce Day weather. She shook him gently.

"Time to wake up."

"What time is it? I must have passed out," he mumbled in a slumber-laden voice.

"You need to shower and get ready. Mama's already here. She brought groceries and cooked brunch."

Corncakes with artisanal cheddar awaited Steele, along with diesel-strength coffee and prickly pear-apple salad punctuated with blueberries. The yellowed envelope, Marika's wax thumbprint sealing the message closed, leaned against the carafe as a centerpiece on the tiny Formica topped table.

"You'll keep this envelope, Thurgood. Let it remain closed, at least until I'm back in Deming."

He sipped the fierce coffee.

Rosa added a corncake to her plate, asking, "Do you think he'll come?" Then, to clarify, "Jacob, I mean?"

"Jake's impulsive, even back then he was; fearsome and erratic. I don't imagine he's changed much. He'll be here if it damn well pleases him, and for no other reason," Marika opined.

"But, isn't that most peoples' motivation, self-interest?" Steele proposed, "Papa lectured me that what seems like altruistic acts really serve for the benefit of the giver—whether they seek to enter into heaven after this life, or believe in karma during this life. Really the same, when you put them side-by-side. Not that Jacob's coming would be altruistic in any sense."

"For us Catholics, what we do here will allow us into heaven—and on the day of judgment into God's eternal grace," Rosa countered, "that's what the Sunday school teachers told us, anyhow."

"Do you still believe it?" Steele wondered.

"I don't know. But karma—why do successful businessmen live well-pampered lives, even though they likely trampled over uncountable people to rise to power?" Rosa questioned.

"It's not just the action, but the intent behind the action. Has your example businessman created a product that improved lives, and profited from his inventiveness?" Steele asked. He thought of Jacob, running a large, successful carnival venture to amuse children and their parents through games, rides, shows, and wondrous acts; was his a pampered life, and what fulfillment did he receive from his work?

"There's the question of free will, as well," Marika pointed out. "I've suffered great, traumatic harm—and caused it too, no doubt; but I have the choice to redirect my actions. The idea of predestined fate is ludicrous—I'm in control of my present and future. I'm not waiting for some god-in-the-clouds to judge me, steer me like some cow destined for eternal laughter or the final slaughter." And today, she knew, she would purge her past. And mangle their lives.

SORT OF CARNIVAL
2000 Twenty-Seven

Marika, Steele, and Rosa circled around the oak table in Charles Dickens, Esquire's sterile meeting room, a collection of obsolete 1988 New York Code and Statutes lining the shelves. Marika's openness the day before eased Steele's tensions—trying to connect her stories with his personal journey afforded a tenuous filament linking them together. Yet the message in the envelope and her insistence on Jacob being present at the legal meeting hovered over him. How did she know of that cabin, and any connections to his family, when Jacob just confirmed it to him also?

Chuck entered, along with an assistant to take notes, his head as shiny as the table's gleam.

"Doctor Steele," he extended his hand, "and you brought your-"

"Girlfriend, Rosa Garcia" Steele said firmly, "and my birth mother, Marika Elizabeth Miller-Garcia."

"Same last name, what a coincidence," Chuck observed.

"She's my mother too," Rosa tossed out, "by adoption, officially."

"So, you're boyfriend/girlfriend and brother/sister?" Chuck rounded out the connections.

"Yes, well—" Steele began.

"Nevermind. Your business, not mine. Will Mr. Jacob Steele join us today? We cannot proceed without him, according to the directive of the late Mr. Levi Steele."

Eyes turned on Steele, who sheepishly shrugged. "We don't know for sure, he was," Steele searched for the diplomatic approach, "unable to fully commit due to another emergency."

A jangle of the door alerted the group to another attendee. The door opened to Darryl Cooper, an aluminum crutch beneath his meaty arm straining to support his mass. "Well, ain't this just the shit," Darryl characteristically bellowed, "how you all doin' today?"

"Why is he here, Mr. Dickens—Chuck?" Steele blurted, confused.

"By the directive of the late Mr. Steele," Chuck answered as if explaining three comes after two.

"But, why? He has no ties to the estate that I know of..." Steele trailed off.

The lawyer responded in his terse manner. "Mr. Cooper assisted the late Mr. Steele as caretaker of the lands in the AFPF trust. Were you not aware?"

Steele stared expressionless. "Caretaker of the AFPF Trust?"

"No more discussion on the topic, not until the remaining required attendee arrives," Chuck stopped.

They waited. Steele wiled his time by willing Jacob to appear and observing the others. The panoramic view of the river and hills to the east captivated Marika, Rosa seemed lost in thought, intermittently rubbing her stomach. Perhaps nerves, or nausea. Occasional vehicles droned through the street below, muffled doors shut closed. Laughter from the street tickled the universe while Darryl's phlegmy breathing sullied the soundscape. The attorney glanced at his watch every forty-five seconds.

Red t-shirt under blue overalls, odors of three days unwashed fumed the cramped space when Jake blazed through the door. His long, slim body and thin facial features held striking similarities with his own, Steele confirmed again. Other than a bloodline, that seemed to be the sole similarity with Steele.

"I ain't got much time, let's get this done. I hope the old man didn't leave me nuthin' cause I don't want any," Jake stated by way of introduction. He scanned the room, noticing Ka and the young Mexican woman beside her, with her black hair pulled into a tight ponytail. "Ka, hello. That your lawyer?"

Steele squeezed Rosa's hand and they interlaced fingers on the table top.

"No, I'm her daughter."

"And his girlfriend?" Jake asked, dismayed, glancing at the boy.

"Right." Chuck started in. "Mr. Levi Steele's instructions clearly stated the division of his estate between—"

Marika stood with anxious defiance, closing down the lawyer. Lancing glares at Jake, she declared, "I've waited my entire adult lifetime for this." She drew a determined breath. And paused just one second longer. "For years I've suppressed the shame, knowing now that as a victim I held no responsibility for what happened." Her eyes pierced Jake deeper.

Marika continued, already feeling lighter. "Do you remember that day, Jake, in 1973 when you dropped me off across from the school? We'd been down to the river, smoking and drinking and making love after skipping out of class? A fisherman floated by, found us naked."

Jake half shrugged and squeaked, "Sounds like most days back then."

"It was April," Marika fleshed out the details. "We'd just fought, you had insulted my parents. After you dropped me off across from the school, you turned the corner and nearly side swiped another car. That was your father."

Nothing registered in Jake's expression, not that Steele could read. Chuck attempted to pull back control, "Ma'am, please sit down so we can begin the bus—,"

"No. I'll not be silenced again," she dismissed him. "These men need to know the full truth." The lawyer glanced at the wall clock.

"He stopped, invited me into his car," her pace quickened, "my body continued to reel from the drugs and alcohol, and I didn't want to explain to the school's front office where I'd been.

So I got in Levi's car. He smelled of camp smoke, which calmed me down after our fight."

Steele listened intently, now envisioning his childhood spent cowering in the silent gaps between shouts. The relationship between Marika and Jacob, obvious now through her outburst, was a glass floor polished with oil. He drifted, imagining himself seven years old in a house with both of them, closing out their yells by creating scenes with action figures and small green army men in Lincoln Logs fortresses. He snapped his attention back to Marika.

Visibly quivering she continued, her voice steady as the river outside. "He drove us out of town, not too far, and said we'd take a short hike. Into the woods, down a small trail barely visible through the brush. I trusted him, he'd always treated me so well. I followed and we talked about our opposition to the war, wishing the end would come soon and the deaths would cease. Finally, we arrived at the cabin. Inside was so cozy, a small bed; the stove still warming the building."

"He turned, locked the door behind him," her voice rippled slightly, she gripped Rosa's shoulder, tears welling in her eyes, venomous memories striking again. "And your father raped me."

The words shattered the room like a grenade in a bucket of nails.

Rosa jumped, hugged Marika, began crying with her. Marika crumbled into her daughter's embrace.

Steele took the blow like an iron mallet to his stomach. He rejected her story outright. The gentle man who raised him couldn't possibly violate anyone—he resisted killing animals that crept into their house. Too much incongruity between the man he loved and the inconceivable accusation. He faintly whispered, "No, that can't be...." Strains of woeful fiddle notes reached him, slightly quelling his reaction.

Jake shrugged and mumbled, "Figures, damn man kept secrets too well," and cast his attention towards the powerful Hudson River.

"And it wasn't the only time," Marika added, wiping tears away with tissue Rosa handed her. "Even when I was pregnant, and living under his roof." Her gaze shifted to Steele, he read pity through her reddened eyes.

Multiple times, Steele wondered? While he grew in utero? Was Levi a serial rapist? Could Papa have been his biological father, not Jacob? Hadn't he preached respect of women, and spoken solemnly of Marika the rare times she came into conversation? His whole upbringing suddenly seemed like some skillfully veiled carnival illusion.

Darryl cleared his throat with a mucus-laced cough. "I seen him go in and out of that cabin. Not seen you." He poked his frankfurter finger towards Marika. "But seen others. A lot of 'em."

Rosa struggled to restrain Marika from leaping across the table at Darryl, "Why didn't you say anything?" Marika demanded.

"He promised me money, promised me a job after high school," Darryl said. "Paid me cash to keep quiet. So I did. Turned out all right for me. Been workin' for him since then."

"You goddamn lunatic." Marika spat out the words with hatred shredding her heart. "You're no better than him." Shock and outrage fueled emotions with the volume escalating, Jacob silently staring out the window the entire time.

Marika's primal physical responses knocked Steele out of his stupor of rejection and befuddlement. And Darryl's corroboration cemented Papa's vile darkness. He forced himself to acknowledge Papa's polar contradictions, at least for the moment. Maybe one day, somehow, he could reconcile the two personas.

Steele noticed Chuck reassessing the document in front of him. Chuck stood, pulling attention back to the original purpose of the gathering. "I have to say, this is a quite unusual day. Most wills are reviewed electronically, it's rare that families gather in person any longer." He drew a deep breath, squeaming slightly uneasily. "In a moment I'll review the final wishes. Keep in mind that by New York intestate law all surviving children of the deceased equally divide anything not included in the will, barring other legal directives.'"

"I don't want none of his stuff—no money, no land, nothin'." Jake hissed and aimed at Steele. "You his kid or grandkid, don't matter to me; take it all."

Chuck read from his notes, Steele only hearing slivers of Chuck's words."…All liquid assets and investments are bequeathed to Thurgood Levi Steele. According to his financial investment team-"

"Team?" Steele interrupted. Did Papa have so much wealth that he employed a team? What other surprises did Papa leave?

"Yes, his team." Chuck continued, beads of sweat accumulating on his glistening head. "His team advised me the value of investments total around one point four million dollars, depending on today's market."

"I told y'all, I don't want none of it," Jake repeated.

Chuck continued without acknowledging Jake. "And the real estate. The AFPF holds legal title to all lands in a revocable trust, save the house on Rimple Road. The house and land are bequeathed to Thurgood Levi Steele. According to the directive, the AFPF transfers holdings and control to the direction of Thurgood Levi Steele."

Steele's shock left him dumbfounded. Paternity, wealth, real estate; the totality confuddled him.

"What does AFPF stand for?" Rosa asked, seemingly the only person listening attentively.

"Well ain't that just the shit, you don't know? Ol' Levi kept a helluva lot of secrets, didn't he?" Darryl tossed out. "It's the Apple Festival and Parade Foundation, for the town of Red Hook. Technic'ly I been workin' for AFPF since forever, keepin' trespassers out." He pointed his hot dog thumbs at Jake and Steele, at opposite ends of the table. "I kicked both you off the land over the years. Levi didn't want no one out there."

"So he could rape young girls," Marika injected, "and you're an accomplice to his barbarity."

"I told you, I seen him take girls in and out. None of my business," Darryl defended himself. "I was just doin' my job." Steele noticed how Marika and Rosa glared loathingly towards

Darryl.

Chuck commanded the room again. "The Trust's holdings encompass four parcels in Red Hook and Rhinebeck, totaling over 830 acres," he paused, "as well as three parcels in Upper Manhattan of two acres total, bordering Lubocci University." He rushed to add, "under separate management, reporting to the trust's board," giving a sideways glance towards Darryl.

Steele's mind remained stuck on the possibility of Levi being his father, and himself a child of rape. Rosa nudged him, whispering, "Did you hear that? Land near your university." Steele vaguely acknowledged her with a slight nod.

"And any remaining property and personal effects not specifically named herein, also to Thurgood Levi Steele," Chuck noted that all taxes and fees could be paid from the estate as well.

"Except," Chuck complicated the situation, "by New York State statutes all biological children may challenge this directive, should any others be identified." Tensions thickened like meat over a high flame.

Jake repeated himself, "I don't want nothin' of his." He found Ka's eyes. "If I'd known what he did to you I'd've beaten the shit out of 'im. No matter he was my father. I loved you then, Ka. But it's been a long, long time. Ain't no excuses, I don't want nothin' that came from that animal." He turned to Chuck. "You write up some papers sayin' I give up any claims to anything, send it to my office and I'll sign." He tossed a crumpled business card from his overall's pocket towards Chuck.

Jake targeted Steele last. "You, you gotta decide if you want all this from a man that raped this woman when she was so young. And so many others. Choice's clear to me, whether he's your dad or granddad, it don't matter." Steele prickled at the ethical dilemma that Jake, in his colloquially loquacious manner, just plopped on the table like a gelatin mold.

Jake continued, "But, we's family anyway it goes. We've lost enough time. I'll be at the Dutchess County Fair later this summer, come find me."

"No key to the midway needed?" Steele asked, a slight smile on his lips.

"And bring her," he pointed to Rosa. "The day's on me."

FIDDLER'S MUSIC
2000 Twenty-Eight

Steele waved the nondescript business envelope for Rosa three weeks later. Tormented by uncertainty about his paternity since Marika revealed her rape left him feeling like an emotional cue ball until he numbed to this moment. What if Papa actually *was* his father? All that youthful angst misdirected at the absent Jacob would have been just phantom growing pains. While not exactly a personable guy, Jacob would deserve some form of apology. But still, the resentment he manifested all those years ago rippled into the tapestry of the man he had become just as the names of the early Dutch settlers echoed in the Hudson Valley today.

"Are you going to open it?" Rosa nudged him as they sat at the kitchen table, plates glazed in remnants of salad dressing and scattered with sunflower seeds, her tight ponytail flipping as she turned her head.

"All this waiting, this not knowing. What will this really change? I am who I am. This fact won't alter anything," Steele said aloud, mostly to himself.

She grabbed the envelope and sliced it open with her finger creating ragged tears, then passed the folded paper back.

Steele stood to walk to the living room, Rosa at his side. He studied the genetic report quietly and matter-of-factly announced, "Papa was my father." His trembling hands telegraphed his inner strife.

"I'm so confused," Steele finally admitted as he collapsed in Papa's overloved, outdated recliner.

Rosa nestled on his lap. "This changes just about everything. There's no more doubting. You were actually raised by one of your parents."

"An evil man who perpetrated horrendous crimes. I'm a consequence of rape. There's no justifying those action. Yet...," yet, here I am, Steele thought. No erasing me.

"I don't condone those actions one iota, he should've been locked away a long time ago," she sneered in disgust. "He clearly loved you, gave you everything needed in this world for your own success," Rosa contradicted herself. "We've had this conversation before. He left a mixed legacy. Detestable, and admirable both. Can one side compensate for, or nullify, the other side? What matters now is what you do with your life, mi amor. And who would have raised you to be the man you are?" She closed, rhetorically.

How could one man be so generous and caring, so publicly endeared; yet so incredibly deceptive and abusive? Which man would Steele honor, the one whose advice propelled him to realize a competitive faculty position at an Ivy League institution? Or the rapist? He carried two of Papa's names, regardless of the DNA.

Antiquated fiddle music visited him, this time clearer than ever. As if the music reached Rosa too, she commanded, "let's go, I want you to show me Fiddler's Bridge. The one you always talk about of That Night. You've promised to take me. Vamonos." Steele agreed, the short drive and the memories would occupy him, some physical movement could lift his mood, and any chance to lecture on local history would be a welcome distraction.

Steele recounted the fiddler's story for Rosa as she pressed for details. What happened to the bride after killing the fiddler? Did she marry again, and was it for love or another arranged union? Did she feel any remorse for placing the blame on her new husband? Was she truly liberated not having to spend her life with him? He ignored the ethics debate she tried to stoke. His own quandary haunted him.

He parked in the café's parking area, noticing a realtor's sign in the well-trimmed grass. They stepped out of the car, turned toward the steel deck bridge they just hummed over, holding each other's hands instinctively, mental images of Chris and Drew and himself as budding teenagers evoking a nostalgic cocktail of loss and comfort.

"Pardon me," a woman's voice called to them as they walked away from the café, "this parking is for customers only."

They turned around, Steele immediately recognizing the woman, Julia. Her hair now fully white, she still held a ponytail with a playful gleam in her eyes.

"It's you, you're back," she smiled at Steele, "you're the kid that was here one night, caused a lot of commotion with the police, as I recall. The fiddler ensorcelled you that night, didn't he?"

"Yes." Steele nodded, amazed she remembered him. "And yes."

"Come inside, please, let's have some coffee. Who is this beauty?" Julia grasped both of Rosa's hands, dipped her forehead towards Rosa's stomach and whispered. "Congratulations, does he know?"

Rosa coyly grinned.

"Or herbal tea, if you prefer," Julia offered.

"What do you remember of the fiddler the night he came to you?" Julia quizzed Steele as they doctored their steaming mugs.

Steele recounted the glowing mass circulating in the unmoving branches and the recorded music Darryl planted under a pile of leaves.

"And since then, any more visits?" Julia dug deeper.

Steele glanced at Rosa. He hadn't mentioned the music to her. "Yes. But only recently. I've lost many important people in my life, and gained others, all within the last month or so. The passing of my oldest friend, Drew, triggered moments of tortuous psychological pain. Then the Fiddler's music returned."

Rosa looked quizzically at Steele, not in frustration at hiding this from her, but weaving the strand to the complex being whose life intertwined with hers long before they first met.

Steele slowly recounted the agony. "That morning after I learned of Drew's passing I curled into a ball, shuttered the windows, and eventually passed out from all the events cascading on me. In the darkest moment strains of fiddle music flittered through my mind. I figured I hallucinated, that first time." He cradled his locally spun mug.

Steel went on. "The next time I heard the faint notes I learned my grandfather might be my father." This confounded Julia. Steele promised to explain later, with a wave of his hand. "Point is, I was fully awake, not dreaming. Then this morning, just before coming out here, I heard the music clearly, as if from the radio."

"He's chosen you," Julia sanctioned. "Once a generation, since his death, he reaches out to someone he identifies with. First time it happened the seasons were turning colder, and the Full Hunter's Moon brightened the sky, seeding the legend of only hearing his music on Halloween. You, and I, know the truth. He selects those who can hear him."

"You've heard this music too, and seen the glow?" Rosa asked skeptically.

"He's always hovering out there in the branches, around the creek," Julia replied. "His melancholy notes have sung for me at low points in my journey. Twice. After the death of my two young children, hit by a drunk driver out in that road one evening many years ago," Julia's eyes softened, her voice quieted. "And when my husband passed away three months ago. The notes vibrate within your soul, dredging the remnants of your zeal for life."

"Yes," Steele agreed. "That's exactly what it's like. It soothes the discomfort."

"As if transforming the pain of death to spark continued life," Julia confirmed.

Steele sipped his coffee, appreciating its heavy, earthy

undertones, considering Julia's interpretation. Each time he'd heard the fiddler—the real fiddler, not Darryl's recording—he had reached a yawning funk, the lowest depths of emotions. The fiddler's notes sparked an uptick in his mood each time, changing his outlook. She captured that pivot point so well.

Julia turned to the subject of the bride who struck the fiddler down. "Do you think the bride regretted her action, killing an innocent man and shifting the blame to her new husband?" The threesome twisted around perspectives, reshaping the event like clay in children's hands. Did the new groom understand she framed him? Did the guilt of two murders fester inside her, or did she embrace her actions as inevitable given her circumstances? Could she be a hero by current values when she shaped her destiny within the strict confines of the traditions and limitations of her culture? The intoxicating ethical debate and historical analysis normalized Steele's disposition.

Julia escorted them to the metal bridge, rust clear along the edges. "Not much to look at, eh? The specific location of where the fiddler crumpled to his death is lost to history, somewhere around here is the best guess we have. It's the biggest bridge, but not the steepest decline for the creek; that's down a ways." She gestured vaguely south.

Steele gauged Rosa, her unenthusiastic response was as he expected. He offered, "The bridge didn't impress us that night, either."

Before departing, Steele requested that Julia remove the sale sign from the yard.

NO REGRETS
2009

"Marika, pick up your toys and see if your brother's awake," Rosa shouted for the third time, "Uncle Jake is stopping by later."

"Will he let us go on the rides again this year?" hoped the eight-year-old.

"Clean up, mija, and don't beg for anything. Abuela will be here soon."

"Students from the camp arrive at ten, where's Inez?" Steele scurried around the kitchen, searching for his replica pipe.

"Last I saw she brought in eggs from the chickens, mi amor. Don't be so worried, you've done this for five years already." Rosa straightened his tunic, tilted his top hat just slightly.

Steele left the house noticing a mortar crack between the stones. He'd get to the repairs soon. They've held for over three hundred years, the house wouldn't crumble in the next couple days. From the perch above the door Lady Liberty's torch upon the blade lit his path as he passed beneath it.

Liza stopped him as he stomped around searching for Inez.

"Bro, hold up. The shelter's outreach coordinator quit yesterday, and the survivors' group meets this afternoon. What we gonna do?"

"You finished your master's in social work, right? You can do this, Liza. Run with it." Steele advised.

With life at full speed, Steele couldn't spend hours and hours replaying *Accelerate*, the latest R.E.M. effort. Its cathartic range of hard electric guitar and lingering synthesized keyboard felt like the natural follow up to New Adventures in Hi-Fi, R.E.M. predictably jolting their dedicated fans with audacious audioscape experiments again. Stipes' voice deepened and lowered over the years, more expressive of a range of emotions to Steele's discerning ear. One lyric rippled through his head as the school bus doors unleashed a stream of middle school children, summing up his life to date:

Realized your fantasies

Are dressed up in travesties

Enjoy yourself with no regrets

ABOUT THE AUTHOR

Shawn J. Woodin left the Empire State for a journey that brought him to the Sunshine State. He started Father, Son, Broken Spirit in the late 1990s in the Peace Corps, and finished it nearly 20 years later after living in three states, returning overseas, earning two graduate degrees, raising two children, and sharing life with his partner. Shawn and his wife, along with their son and daughter, live and meditate in Florida.

Made in the USA
Monee, IL
03 October 2022

15114110R00129